BAD SANTA

Kiru Taye

First Published in Great Britain in 2021 by
LOVE AFRICA PRESS
103 Reaver House, 12 East Street, Epsom KT17 1HX
www.loveafricapress.com

Available in eBook and paperback format

YADILI SERIES

<u>Prince of Hearts</u>
<u>Killer of Kings</u>
<u>Bad Santa</u>
<u>Rough Diamond</u>
<u>Tough Alliance</u>

Kiru Taye

BAD SANTA

BLURB

Although Gina Badu is a good girl all-year-round, she knows her Christmas wish will never come true. Not with a recent divorce, late parents and a sister who courts trouble. Then Santa abducts her in the middle of the night. Except this Santa is terrible—a silver fox of a tattooed fallen angel.

Osagie Peters is a ruthless, cartel boss whose dark soul threatens to consume her. He scares her as much as he fascinates her. It seems he's got her on the naughty list. Still, there's a chance she might have a Merry Christmas after all.

Celebrate the festive season Yadili style. Osagie: Bad Santa is an Yadili series romantic suspense novella and is the prequel to Osagie: King of Clubs. Osagie was first introduced in Xandra: Killer of Kings, Yadili series book 2.

Content warning: kidnapping.

ONE

"SIR, THE PARTY PLANNER, for the Odilis' New Year's Eve dinner party, wants to know if you will have an escort. She is finalising numbers and seating arrangements. What should I tell her?"

It took two words to ruin Osagie Peters' day.

Party planner and dinner party. Actually, four damned words but hey, he could be excused for miscounting.

He didn't have a university degree, as some people liked to remind him. Polite society didn't want him. But they loved the taxes he paid, loved that he employed people, and loved that his businesses attracted visitors, contributing to local tourism and the economy.

Nicknamed the 'King of Clubs', Osagie owned the most popular party venue in the country and perhaps, the African continent.

Club Arufin was the crown jewel in his nightclubs chain, and almost a million partygoers walked through the doors annually. He controlled one hundred franchisees and many more associates. Anyone who wanted to run a successful club in the region paid dues to him.

Yet, the word 'party' might as well be a trigger. Mention it in Osagie's presence and his stomach clenched hard, while his body temperature elevated.

He maintained outwardly calm at his assistant, Remi's question.

He had no problem with the upcoming event.

Duke Odili was the new boss in town. Almost a year ago he'd eliminated John Bull Owo and his son Marlon in a cartel war, married the Owo heiress, Carla and taken over the Owo operations in Lori Osa and surrounding regions. He'd ascended into the head of the Odili family's position in the megacity, a coveted rank in the Yadili network.

With Duke's promotion from 'Underboss' to 'Boss', he'd extended a hand of friendship to Osagie. They were working on an alliance that would protect their interests and expand their reaches.

To Osagie's knowledge, the party was Duke's way of cementing the new alliances. He would need them to survive in the shark-infested waters of doing business in Lori Osa.

Although Osagie was at least fifteen years older than Duke, he appreciated the invitation and respected the man. In this game, age meant jack all. What mattered was the clout, connections, and cash a person brought to a deal. Duke had all three, and as the son of a late statesman, he was also political nobility.

However, the event drew a twinge of discomfort, reminding Osagie of his one regret—he didn't have his family close. Or rather, what should have been his family.

More specifically, his son.

His ex-wife, though. She could burn in Hell, after what she did to him. She was lucky not to have become a late wife.

He had no illusions about the kind of person he was. He was not a nice man. He'd been on Santa's naughty list for too many years.

However, he could never live with himself if he'd hurt the mother of his child.

Not even after he'd caught her in bed with another man.

She'd begged for her life. Her excuse had been that he wasn't educated and her family hadn't approved of him because of it. She'd felt under pressure and had succumbed to the affair with another man.

Educated ko, pressure ni, as his half-Yoruba business partner had said in disdain at the time.

What about his love for her, his willingness to do anything for her?

What about her loving him back, and telling her snobbish family to go to Blazes?

As an orphan, he'd wanted a family of his own so much. He would have done anything to provide for and protect them. He'd been young and stupid enough to believe that a woman from a different background would return his affection.

Instead of love, she'd betrayed him and taught him valuable lessons. He would never be good enough for polite society, so why bother trying to appease them.

Instead of slitting hers and her lover's throats, he'd walked out of the house and divorced her.

She'd remarried and had more children.

He would've loved to keep Odigie, his eighteen-month-old son, with him. Still, he'd accepted the boy had been too young to be without his mother at the time.

That had been twenty years ago.

In the early years of their separation, they'd rotated who had custody during the summer, Easter, and Christmas holidays. He never missed birthdays or special occasions if he could help it.

Now Odigie was old enough to choose where he wanted to spend his holidays. The boy hadn't mentioned if he would visit soon, although they communicated regularly via facetime.

Osagie wouldn't dictate or beg for a visit. If his son preferred to spend the festive season with his other family, so be it.

It didn't stop the hollowness in his chest or the fatigue descending on him. He didn't feel sociable or interested in parties.

As for female companionship, while there'd been sexual encounters, he hadn't entertained any candidates for the next Mrs Peters. He wouldn't give his heart away again.

Instead, he'd sunken his time and energy into running his businesses both legit and not-so-legit. He had neither the time nor the inclination to keep a steady lover.

"Sir?" Remi's tentative voice pulled him from his reverie.

"Tell her I'll have a companion." His contact list was full of options.

The sound of the opening door caught Osagie's attention.

Idehen Cruz walked in, his expression grim, and his voice gruff. "Remi, excuse us."

Osagie rubbed his hand on his temple. His friend's countenance didn't bode well, and Osagie wasn't in the mood for any bad news.

Remi shifted in the leather chair across the desk, eyes widened and alarmed. "Will that be all, sir?"

"Yes, thank you," he said, glad he'd already given out instructions before his friend's arrival. He lifted the bottle of water and poured into a glass, sipping the cold liquid before taking a deep calming breath.

The woman looked uncomfortable as she packed up the folder and retreated hastily.

Osagie stared at his oldest friend and business partner who marched to-and-fro, at risk of burning a path through the hard-wearing carpet.

Just like Osagie, Idehen had started greying and had trimmed white facial hair against umber skin. But unlike him, his friend had a completely shaved head while Osagie had a shock of salt and pepper hair he kept cut almost to the scalp. His eyes were whisky-brown compared to Osagie's midnight-black.

Idehen was a formidable figure, broad-shouldered and at over six feet. Yet, he was generally the more mellow of the two friends, the one who made silly jokes. One of the few people who could make Osagie laugh.

Osagie was the one often described as unapproachable, the cold, calculating one and people scurried away from him before he'd even spoken.

But Idehen's warm and jovial appearance could be deceptive. Like a hurricane, he had the power to cut down a mob of men in a fight.

And right now, Idehen moved like a tornado.

They had been homeless street boys who had fought and stolen for survival, for the food in their bellies, the clothes on their back, even the places they'd lain their heads. They had been each other's keepers. Even taken care of other vulnerable children around them.

Over the years, Osagie had learned to adapt and evolve with the times like a chameleon. The key to his survival and staying relevant in an ever-changing world.

He couldn't remember stepping into a classroom. Everything he'd learned had been self-taught. He'd spent most of his youth at internet cafes, reading, learning and, of course, grifting.

Idehen had been by his side through it all. A combination of savvy brain and quick-footed brawn had kept them not entirely on the right side of polite society and yet not hardcore enough to be excluded totally.

Now, Osagie grabbed glasses and a cognac bottle. He strode through a door behind his desk. The soundproof private lounge provided a haven in the bustle of a busy enterprise.

He lowered the items on the dark wood, low table, removed the tailor-made jacket of his charcoal suit, hung it over the arm of the sofa and sank into the worn leather sofa.

Idehen followed, the door slamming behind him.

"What's the bad news?" Osagie poured the dark-amber liquor into the tumblers.

His friend said nothing for a few seconds that stretched painfully.

"We've been hacked," Idehen said finally, his voice gruff as if he'd been shouting all day.

"Hacked?" Osagie lifted his eyebrow and tilted his head.

"Yes. Someone hacked into our system and wired money out of one of the accounts."

Osagie said nothing while he processed the information. This wasn't the first time someone had attempted to defraud them. It came with the territory. However, not many people were brave enough to try it in the first place because the consequences were dire.

Osagie did not forgive. He'd used up his forgiveness quota on his ex-wife.

Anyone who slighted him was punished heavily. Painfully.

"How much?" he asked, running his finger around the rim of the short glass. It helped to calm him and kept his head clear of emotions.

"Ten thousand dollars."

He didn't flinch. It wasn't the first time they'd lost money. Still, it was large enough to require a hefty penalty. He couldn't ignore it.

"How was this possible?"

Idehen balled his hand into fists. "The accounting and IT teams have felt my rage already. I think it was an internal job. One member of the team wasn't at work today."

Osagie could imagine that Idehen had blazed through the accounting team and the IT guys. Whatever the loophole would be fixed.

"Who?"

"Dani. Daniella Badu." Idehen pulled out a digital device from his pocket, tapped on the screen and slid it across the table.

Osagie picked it and stared at the photo of a woman posted on social media.

She was a software developer in the IT department. The shot was of her in a pouty selfie with heavy makeup and long hair extensions. She looked like she was performing for the camera, for an audience.

The consequence of stealing from him was severe. The staff knew him.

Yet this one had dared to try. She wouldn't get away with it. If she did, others would think he had gone soft and try to steal more. And there would be those who would even attempt to take over his operations, which meant his death.

He took another sip of cognac and placed the glass on the table. His movements were precise and smooth, his expression blank.

"Find her." His voice was cold.

He tapped the screen again, and another photo showed up. A different woman in a crop sports top and leggings stared at him from a reclined position on a yoga mat.

Something fluttered in his chest. "Hang on. Who's this?"

He tapped on the screen to read the birthday post from earlier in the month.

This was Daniella's sister? And she'd recently turned forty years old?

The woman was stunning—oval face, brown eyes, cinnamon skin, toned abs, lean-fit body that didn't look a day over thirty. Even the long dark hair parted in the middle and packed into two low buns added a touch of cuteness.

Perfection.

Mouth moistening, he gaped at the photo, momentarily forgetting his anger at the missing money.

Idehen leaned across the table to look at the picture. "That's Dani's sister, Gina."

"Yes, I read the post," Osagie replied, annoyed at the effect the woman's image seemed to have on him.

The sisters probably colluded to defraud him and were out there, right now, spending his money and laughing at him.

His interest should be in recovering the funds and punishing the culprits. Not ogling one of the suspects, no matter how fine she was.

"The two live together down in Daware," Idehen said, lifting the drink to his lips.

"Then find both of them." Osagie pushed the phone across the table towards his friend.

***

"Tell me again why we're doing this instead of sending the boys to handle it?" Idehen asked, two days later, as he parked the SUV on a quiet residential street and killed the engine.

Good question.

Osagie sat in the front passenger seat. Still dark, they had driven about an hour across the city to this estate in the Daware suburb. Now, the sky was dawn grey, neither dark nor light.

They could have sent others. Their boys had investigated and reported that Daniella was nowhere to be found. Her sister, however, was here. The next step would have been to instruct the boys to take and secure the sibling until Daniella was located.

He'd imagined his men maltreating Georgina—apparently, that was Gina's full name which he preferred—and his blood had run cold.

He didn't want her injured in the process. Regardless of her status as Daniella's sister, he had no proof of her direct involvement.

The hacking and theft incidents weren't the end of the world. But it could mark the beginning of the end for Osagie. If he didn't catch and punish the culprits severely, many more thefts would follow. He had no doubt employees, and others were watching and waiting to see his response.

Mostly since there were women involved this time.

He wasn't in the business of harming the innocent. He'd sworn to adhere to certain principles no matter what—protect the weak, and touch not the innocent were two codes he stuck to amongst others.

Georgina wasn't weak. He'd watched some of her fitness videos on social media. The woman was physically and mentally strong, no doubt. However, until he could ascertain her involvement, he would treat her as an innocent—someone outside of his tainted world.

So, the only people he trusted with her welfare were in this car right now.

"Some jobs are best done yourself," Osagie rationalised.

"Mmhmm." His friend didn't sound convinced. "Is that the only reason?"

Osagie's face tingled. He stiffened, annoyed for feeling like the hungry boy caught trying to steal food.

Perhaps he shouldn't be concerned about the woman's welfare. Still, he had no reason to feel embarrassed for trying to protect an innocent. Once Dani was found, he had no business sitting in the car outside the woman's house.

"What other reason is there? If they mess it up, we don't get our money back."

"Just saying." Idehen shook his head as a grin split his face. "We became big men, so others can do this kind of shit."

"Big men, huh?" His friend's humour made Osagie chuckle. "Seriously though, don't you miss this?"

"This?" His friend turned to look at him.

"Yes, this." Osagie waved his hand to indicate their current situation. "The thrill of the hustle. Picking a mark, planning, and executing the score. Avoiding detection."

"Sometimes, I miss it. But we were struggling for survival in those days. This is not the same thing. This is a matter of respect and that Dani woman needs a serious lesson in respect. You don't spit in your fucking eating bowl."

His friend's outburst sparked questions in Osagie. Was there more going on than Idehen had revealed?

Before he could ask, movement across the street distracted him. His pulse rate spiked, and he leaned forward.

The metal pedestrian gate to Georgina's two-bedroom ground-floor apartment building cranked open.

"Here we go," Idehen muttered.

Georgina came out, dressed in another crop sports top and leggings combo with brightly coloured trainers, hair in a low bun. She pulled the barrier shut and jogged along the pavement of the hundred-residence Highgate Estate. Her running shoes pounded the tarmac as she headed across the road, squeezing between parked cars to go toward the field.

"Check out the apartment. See if there's anything that indicates where her sister's gone. I'll follow her and let you know when she heads back." Osagie reached for the door and stepped out.

"Right." Idehen exited the car, clicking the fob to lock it. "Happy hunting."

Osagie grinned at the old remark. They used to say that to each other when they were younger men hustling for pay-days. He tugged the hood of the black long-sleeved jersey over his head and entered the park.

Ahead, trees stood as unmoving sentries and bushes demarcated the adventure playground's shadows from the ghost mist hovering over the sizeable glittering pond. A chilly Harmattan breeze whipped dust and the leaves in the trees.

It was damned cold. His head-to-toe kit provided cover, and the run would warm him up. Still, he would rather jog on a treadmill than exercise with the sand in his eyes.

It seemed Georgina preferred the opposite. She co-owned a gymnasium not far from here. Yet, according to the report he'd received, she used the park at dawn daily, adding to the things about her that fascinated him.

Hence the reason he was braving the brisk weather on a December morning. He kept his distance from her, staying out of sight until he got the lay of the park. He expected more people, joggers, dog-walkers, or people just cutting-through to different destinations.

However, after ten minutes, he spotted only one other person. Perhaps, the regular users had travelled for the festivities since it was less than a week until Christmas.

Keeping to the open space, Georgina completed two laps before she paused to stretch her warmed muscles. Then she continued her third lap. Her movement was fluid and entrancing, the strides of an athlete.

He took advantage of the deserted location and headed in her direction but maintained the gap.

As if she sensed his presence, she glanced back.

His drab black outfit would make him appear indistinguishable in the grey light and with the distance. He wore long-sleeves to hide his tattoos. Only his face and hands were visible.

Hopefully, if Idehen found her sister's location, he wouldn't have to contact Georgina.

And Osagie would be rid of this constant lust. From the moment he'd seen her photo on Idehen's phone, she'd lit a fire in his veins.

But Georgina looked too sweet and clean for his twisted life. And he didn't fuck around with lovely and naïve. So yes, he was keeping his distance.

He was only here because she may have colluded with her sister to steal from him. He had to keep his mind on the goal.

Georgina gave him a second curious look. Then she turned away, adjusted her earbuds, fiddled with the phone attached to a pack on her back and increased her running speed. She did another set of laps, avoiding the dark, dense foliage of trees.

She disappeared behind some shrubs, and he stayed back, not wanting to spook her. Or make her return home too early. Idehen needed time to search the house.

Someone should have warned her about wearing headsets while running in a secluded park before sunrise. She didn't know who could be lurking about like he was, even if this was supposed to be a secure neighbourhood.

After five more laps, she slowed down, pulled a water bottle from the pack's latch, and took a drink.

Watching her throat ripple as she drank made him thirst, for cool refreshing water, for the salty taste of her skin.

Damn, he had it bad.

Putting the bottle aside, she took a couple of steps and stumbled.

Unable to keep away, he sprinted towards her, discarding caution.

She spread her arms, righting herself. Then she froze and stared at him with genuine appreciation until he stopped beside her.

"Are you okay?" he asked, his voice unexpectedly husky.

He searched her face, checking her over. He couldn't explain this need to be near her. To make sure she was unharmed.

Up close, her photos didn't convey her brilliance.

Although he was taller and worked out regularly at the gym, she outclassed him. Her ripped abs alone could put him to shame.

She was beautiful and knowledgeable. He'd discovered she was studying for a Master programme. He hadn't even finished secondary school.

Not to mention that he was older and she looked like she would look great with one of those younger celebrities hanging off her arm.

She was a goddess.

He was in awe and would die to worship at her altar even for one night.

Swallowing hard, she bobbed her head, as if unable to work saliva into her mouth. Sheens of sweat beaded her deep-arched brows and the top of her bow-shaped lips.

She opened her mouth and closed it, seeming to struggle with breathing. Her body swayed.

"You don't look well. Lean forward," he instructed and reached out, hand sliding over her shoulder gently. "Breathe deep."

She leaned in, gulping air.

"Have a drink." He stepped close, reached for her pack, and withdrew the bottle of water. In protective mode, his actions were without timidity or uneasiness.

"I'm all right." She took the bottle off him and drank. Then she looked up at his face, scrutinising him. "Do I know you?"

"No." His heart raced. He shouldn't have come this close. Now that she'd seen his face, she might be able to identify him later.

Footsteps made him turn.

A man in a Tee and shorts set slowed his jogging and marked time beside them.

"Gina, are you all right?" the stranger asked, staring at her and then at the Osagie.

Osagie's spine stiffened, and his jaw tightened. Who was the man?

"Hi, Bob. I'm okay," she replied after drawing in a shaky breath. She glanced at the Osagie and said, "I have to go."

His expression remained inscrutable, but he nodded at her.

She ran off with the Bob guy.

Osagie pulled his phone from his pocket and sent a message to Idehen.

She's heading home. One minute.

He jogged towards the car.

Idehen already sat at the driver's seat with a scowl on his face.

"What's up?" Osagie asked as he got in.

"Can you imagine? The woman is in Dubai, spending our money. I'm going to strangle her when I get my hands on her."

Osagie chuckled. He'd never seen his friend so frustrated, certainly not over any woman. "It sounds to me like you want to do more than strangle Daniella. Is there something going on between you two?"

Idehen jerked back, looking affronted. "Of course, there's nothing between that troublesome woman and me. The last time she came to me, batting her long lashes, asking for some time off. And then the money went missing the next day."

"And now you want to strangle her."

"Yes!"

"I didn't know you were into erotic asphyxiation."

"What?" Idehen did the backward jerk again, eyes bulging in a comical expression.

"Gotcha." Osagie laughed out loud. "You should see your face."

"Bastard." His friend shook his head, lips curving upwards.

"And they say I don't crack jokes." Osagie sobered when someone came out of Gina's building. "There's a complication. Georgina saw my face."

The plan had been simple.

Locate the culprits—Daniella and accomplices. Recover the cash. Mete out the punishment. Avoid collateral damage—Georgina, specifically.

Now it seemed they had an inadvertent casualty.

Idehen scrubbed a palm over his face and puffed out air. "We can't leave her. We don't want her warning Dani that we're onto her."

"I know." Osagie sighed. "This is turning into one big party."

Except they didn't laugh at the joke because it meant the one thing he'd wanted to avoid—taking a hostage. Taking Georgina.

TWO

WHEN IT RAINED, it poured.

The saying reflected Gina Badu's life and more specifically today.

It seemed her mobile phone hadn't stopped vibrating all day like it was currently doing in her jeans' back pocket as she inserted the key into the lock of her front door. Her hands were full of grocery bags, so she couldn't reach the gadget immediately.

Last night's sleep had been rough. This morning she'd hoped to shake off the heaviness in her chest with a run in the park. A dizzy spell and a brief encounter with a sexy stranger had added to her sense of foreboding.

She'd returned home, showered, dressed, and eaten a quick breakfast. Afterwards, she'd made the ten-minute trip to MG Fitness, which was the gymnasium she co-owned with business partner Mike Ogueri.

The troubles had started as soon as she'd arrived in the building. First had been a plumbing problem which meant the shower room had to be closed temporarily and had taken all day to fix. Then, she'd had to deal with a supplier's complaint about an outstanding invoice.

Mike usually dealt with suppliers. He'd travelled for the holidays and had been unreachable when she'd tried to contact him. Network problems, she assumed.

Gina had apologised to the supplier and promised to settle the outstanding bill.

Luckily, it had been a quiet day, with regards to customers.

As Christmas fast approached, members would rather party than spend their spare moments in a spin class or lifting weights. Sure, the hardcore regulars showed up. However, the general motto around here seemed to be 'party in December, repent in January.' New membership registrations and attendances usually surged with New Year resolutions to keep active.

Once the lock clicked, she shoved the slab with shoulders, stepped across the threshold, and kicked the door shut. She nudged the switch on the wall. Bright light filled the hallway as she hurried towards the kitchen.

The two-bed apartment was one of many residences in the new Highgate Estate of Daware Town on Lori Osa's outskirts. Gina and her sister Dani moved into the area less than a year ago after her mother's funeral.

Pain flared in the back of Gina's throat. Their family had been closely-knit, and the loss of two parents had been difficult for both women.

Gina had channelled her grief into building the fitness training partnership she'd invested her savings. As a retired professional athlete, she worked as a fitness model. She also studied part-time for a Master's degree in sports therapy.

Dumping the bags on the vinyl kitchen floor, she reached for the phone and pulled it straight to her ear as she clicked to answer. It was probably Mike returning her calls.

"Hey, sis," the female voice greeted.

"Dani!" A rush of warmth spread across Gina's chest as she straightened, pleased to hear her sister's voice after two days. "How are you? Did you get my message?"

"Yes, I saw it. I'm fine. How are you?"

"You won't believe the kind of crazy day I've had."

"Oh. What happened? Are you okay?"

"Yes, I'm fine. It's just that we had a leak in the changing rooms at the gym and I spent most of the day dealing with plumbers. But it's sorted now."

"I'm sorry you had to deal with that stress. Why don't you just close the gym until after Christmas? Mike isn't there anyway."

"I can't shut the place down. Some people use the gym daily."

"Come on, sis. We both know that closing the place for a few days won't be the end of the world. You haven't had a break for a long time. Not since..." her sister trailed off.

Gina stared out of the window, barely noticing the security-lit passage and grey wall. She knew what Dani omitted.

Gina hadn't had time off work for a long time. Not since their mother's funeral.

Even that hadn't been a break. The stress of planning the funeral and dealing with the aftermath had made going back to work feel like a holiday.

Still, work was the only thing keeping her together, keeping her sane. Doing nothing wasn't an option she wanted to explore right now.

"I'll be fine. I'm getting two days off over Christmas." The time she'd set aside for studying. Feeling uncomfortable, she changed the subject. "How is Dubai?"

Leaning against the counter, she crossed one arm over her chest, the other holding the phone up.

Dani sighed. "Sis, listen. If it's the money you're worried about, don't be. I have some cash coming soon, so I can cover the expense of you taking a holiday."

"It's not about the money." A cold finger slithered down Gina's back. "Hang on. How come you suddenly have the cash to splash?"

Dani was frivolous and had no savings, although she worked as a computer programmer and earned a decent wage.

Gina had been surprised she could afford a trip to Dubai, considering Dani had bought the ticket last minute. She'd thought it had been a treat from Dani's boyfriend.

"It's just a side hustle that paid off." Dani didn't sound bothered.

Made sense. Around here, everyone had side hustles to make ends meet.

Her sister deserved the vacation after the stresses of the past few years. They'd cared for their sick mother, who'd subsequently lost her battle with cancer.

If Gina hadn't sunken her money on the gymnasium and tuition fees, maybe she could have gone on the trip with her sister.

"So, what have you got planned? Sightseeing and shopping?"

"That's the plan."

"What's the matter? You don't sound happy?"

Dani sighed. "It's Bolaji. I can't reach him."

Gina straightened. "What do you mean, you can't reach him? Isn't he in Dubai with you?"

Bolaji was Dani's boyfriend of a few months. They'd met about six months ago, and things had moved quickly between them.

The sisters had their fair share of destructive relationships. However, Bolaji seemed to be one of the good guys, and Dani had fallen hard for him.

"We didn't travel together," Dani said, sounding frustrated. "He was supposed to come the day after. His flight arrived, but I haven't seen him. I've been trying his phone, and it's not connecting."

"Oh." Something niggled at the back of Gina's mind. "Bolaji must be on the way to you, and his phone is dead. He knows which hotel you're in, right?"

"Yes. He knows the hotel details. I'm just concerned because I can't reach him. Will you do me a favour?"

"Sure. What do you need?"

"Call his number and see if you can get to him, please. Find out where he is."

"Sure. I can call him now and message you back."

"Okay. But before you go. Has anyone been asking about me?"

"Anyone like whom?"

"Just anyone. You know what, don't worry about it."

A sick feeling settled in Gina's stomach. Her sister didn't sound okay. "Is something wrong?"

"Of course, nothing is wrong," Dani sounded defensive. "Just call Bolaji. Please."

"Fine. I'll contact him and call you back."

"Okay. Speak to you shortly."

Gina cut the call and scrolled through her messages for the one where Dani had sent Bolaji's phone number months ago when the two of them started dating. They always shared contact for new boyfriends just in case of emergencies. There were too many psychos walking the earth.

She pressed the dial button, and the number rang without response. After trying a second time, she called her sister back.

"Sorry. There was no answer," she said when Dani replied.

"Where the Hell is he? I swear to God. If he's still in Nigeria, this won't be funny."

Something still didn't feel right about this, and Gina asked, "Did Bolaji pay for the flight?"

"No. I booked the flights and hotel. Then at the last minute, Bolaji said something came up, and he had to go see his mother but would join me on the next available flight."

"Oh. So, you paid for his flight?"

"At first, yes, until he changed the date. He is going to reimburse me and pay for the shopping. If he ever gets here."

"Of course, he'll get there. He might have been delayed. Just be patient."

Dani puffed out air. "Yeah. I know. I'm trying to be. He better hurry. I want to get out of this room. This trip was supposed to be lit, you know."

"It will be fun. But I'm curious. How could you afford to pay for it all?"

"I told you I had a deal that came through," Dani said nonchalantly.

"A deal. What kind of deal? Hope nothing dodgy."

"Seriously, you should loosen up. You always jump to conclusions, sis."

"You know I have reasons. I worry about you."

Dani had form. As a teenager, she'd once hacked into the state government pension systems and automatically sent cheque payments to all the retired civil service pensioners. A favourite uncle had complained he hadn't received his pension for months. Meanwhile, the governor had been spending money on useless monuments.

Dani had been arrested. Luckily, their father, who'd been an influential lawyer, had managed to get the case dropped. Dani had been sixteen. The governor didn't want the media uproar that would prevent his re-election. He made a speech, stating the payments hadn't been an error, after all.

Pensioners got their money. Dani didn't go to jail. The state governor got re-elected.

A win for all made possible by their brilliant father who'd doted on Gina.

"Gosh, I miss dad and mum." Her chest squeezed tight and a lump lodged in her throat.

"Me too, sis," Dani said solemnly. There was silence on the line for a few seconds. "We're going to be okay, you know. Both of us."

"I know." Gina rubbed a hand over her face and tilted her head against the high cupboard. They would be okay. They were both adults, and life went on, regardless. Dani was her last surviving close relative, and she didn't want to lose another so soon. "Take care of yourself."

"Will do. You, too." Dani hesitated.

"Sure. Let me know when Bolaji arrives."

"I will. Bye, sis."

"Bye." Gina sighed as she ended the call.

The prickly sensation on Gina's nape remained though. Sighing, she walked into the living room and turned on the fairy lights. The decorated Christmas tree glittered with tinsel and baubles.

She'd rescued the old tree from her late parents' home. She couldn't bear to throw it away.

They'd had a strong family unit, and during the festive season, they were always together. When she'd been a kid, she'd loved travelling to her hometown with her parents for the festivals when citizens at home and abroad would return to their ancestral homes.

Even as adults, they'd spent Christmas with her mother after her father died from a car crash, except for some years during Gina's brief marriage.

Shaking her head, she dismissed the thought of her ex. He didn't deserve space in her head.

She only wished she could recreate the same holiday spirit she'd enjoyed when her parents were alive. But Christmas would never be the same without her mother. Her sister seemed to have her own plans, anyway.

She stared at the tree blankly unable to shift the heaviness settling like stones in her gut.

Her life was busy and monotonous, consisting of the business, schoolwork, training and sleeping.

Her stomach growled as if to remind her there was another activity she omitted. Of course, she ate somewhere in between all the other things going on. But sometimes in a rush to get about she survived on energy bars.

She couldn't remember the last time she'd just chilled out or even partied.

Swivelling, she returned to the kitchen, stored the groceries before making a quick bite to eat.

She sat in front of the TV while browsing social media. Afterwards, she showered and got into bed. It would be another busy day tomorrow.

***

Something woke Gina in the middle of the night. She didn't dream a lot, and she rarely had nightmares.

Opening her eyes, she stared up at the ceiling in the gloom. Yellow light from the streetlamp streaked in weakly. The estate had its own power generation which stayed on twenty-four-seven.

She didn't like having the AC on at night, so she kept the window open to get as much air in as possible. It didn't help. The cotton T-shirt she slept in clung damply to her breasts.

"Hello, Georgina," a rumbling voice spoke in the darkness.

She bolted upright, heart thudding, her eyes scanning the darkness.

Nobody used her full name except her parents. They'd been expecting a boy before she'd been born and would have named him George. She'd turned up. Hence Georgina.

However, these days, she introduced herself as Gina. And since she didn't believe in ghosts, her parents were not in her apartment right now.

"Who's that?"

A shadow moved forward at the foot of the bed, and she reached for the light switch.

"Don't do that." The voice was low and rumbling, a warning.

Her hand froze mid-air, and she pulled it back.

Did it matter if she saw the face of the person who was about to murder her in bed?

From the silhouette, the person was tall, broad and in dark clothing. The voice was deep enough to be masculine. The cut and shimmer of the jacket identified that he wore a suit.

"Who are you?" She swallowed. Her throat had gone dry, and her voice sounded sharp.

"My name is Osagie," he replied in a wonderfully rich timbre, velvety and chocolaty.

Something in his deep voice had a weirdly calming effect, considering the situation.

She should've been freaking out at having a stranger in her room in the middle of the night. Instead, the almost familiar, rich quality of his voice fascinated her.

What the fuck was wrong with her?

"I don't want you to panic," he continued.

A cold finger of fear slithered down her spine, triggering her fight or flight mode.

"I shouldn't panic. Are you freaking kidding me right now? There's a stranger in my house, and he's telling me not to panic—"

"Georgina."

Shit. The calm way he said her name was both sexy and threatening.

Clamping her mouth shut, she held her breath, trying to calm her racing heart. She'd probably pissed him off. When she was agitated, she talked a lot, a natural response.

He stepped forward so that the weak light from the window hit one side of his face.

Recognition dawned on her. She'd seen that face before. Seen him. This morning.

Mr Sexy and Dangerous.

The man in black.

The memory played.

She was running in the park as was her daily routine when the skin on her neck prickled, and she glanced back. Her heart took up a sudden staccato beat.

A man in an all-black outfit ran behind her, about one hundred metres away and made no effort to close the distance. She'd never seen him in the park before. Certainly not one of the neighbours. Usually, news of arrivals spread quickly in the area where local gossip was rife.

She ignored him and continued running. When she had a dizzy spell and stumbled, he approached her.

He wore a long-sleeve jersey with a hood and full-length track bottoms, which covered his entire body aside from his face. Beneath the black hood, a hardened face with symmetrical features loomed over. He had straight, thick brows over those striking eyes.

And sensuous lips that made her think of fallen angels.

He sounded concerned as he helped her until Bob, one of her neighbours, arrived, and the man's jaw hardened as if he didn't like Bob. She'd made an excuse and jogged home.

However, she had been unable to shake the man's image from her mind.

And what a striking face—caramel skin, rugged features, silver-grey beard on this chin that made him look like Santa Claus. Piercing eyes intent on her. Like a predator tracking prey, he exuded danger.

A shiver of pleasure ran down her spine as her core clenched. Okay, she had a thing for bearded men, and this silver fox was precisely her cup of coffee.

Now, the same man stood in her bedroom looking as menacing as ever.

Her muscles went rigid as she realised that the look she'd seen in his eyes this morning had been a veiled promise—he'd see her again.

He'd come here for her.

Shit! The hairs on her nape and arms lifted. Her gaze bounced around the room, and her mind worked fast, calculating how to get away.

"Get out of my house!" she shouted.

"I won't warn you again," he replied in a smooth voice.

To Hell with his warning. She wasn't staying to find out his intentions.

She bolted off the bed, and through the open door. She was an athlete, and running was her speciality. She couldn't fight him. He was bigger, taller, and broader. Still, she could outrun him.

This was her apartment. She knew the layout better than him.

She sprinted down the hallway. It didn't matter that she was barefooted and in her sleep shorts and top. If she could get out of the front door, there was a chance of one of her neighbours overhearing the noise and intervening. Or at least, someone would call the police.

Reaching the entrance, she clicked the lock and twisted the handle in her hand.

Arms banded around her, imprisoning her. There was a second man. How many others were there?

She kicked out and screamed just as hands covered her mouth. A needle pricked her neck. Dizziness overcame her.

"Be careful with her."

She heard the warning from Osagie before she blanked out.

***

The light hurt her eyes when she opened them. Feeling disorientated, she squeezed them shut, and let out a moan. A marching band seemed to be having a festival in her head.

Did she drink alcohol last night? Not possible since she worked all the time and hadn't been partying in ages.

Snatches of yesterday flashed through her mind.

Dani's call. The man in black. In the park. In her room.

Osagie.

Her eyes flew open, and she sat upright in bed. Not her bed.

She glanced around the space. Not her apartment.

Light from the rising sun beamed through floor-to-ceiling windows into what could only be described as a beautiful bedroom—magnolia walls, furnishings in warm colours and a large bed with luxurious, soft, white sheets.

Did Osagie abduct her?

"I won't warn you again."

Remembering his words made her shiver. She rubbed her arms as her feet hit the thick-piled carpet. She still wore the clothes from last night. Had it been last night?

With quick steps, she reached the first door and turned the handle, which didn't budge.

She repeated the action with the other doors. One was a closet filled with women's clothes.

The other was a bathroom with a sophisticated shower unit, light grey limestone tiles covered the walls and floor, a white sink, and a glass shelf with a plastic toothbrush and tube of toothpaste.

Locked in. She had no obvious way of getting out.

Blinking rapidly, she walked stiffly over to the barricaded window. She was surrounded by sprawling greenery of manicured lawn and flowering plants and mature trees. Further down was high fencing.

Whoever lived here was extraordinarily rich.

A wave of dizziness hit her, and she stumbled back. Mouth agape, her hands turned clammy, and her knees weakened.

She couldn't very well climb out of this window. Imagining being stuck in here for however long congealed her belly into stone. She turned her back to the optimistic view.

She wasn't chained and locked in a dingy dungeon. Still, this ivory tower stood as her prison. She couldn't escape it.

Who was Osagie, and why had he abducted her? The place reeked of money. Did he make his money from kidnapping people?

A clicking sound made her stiffen and turn to the locked door. It swung inward.

A huge man in black Tee and black slacks entered. With an aluminium tray in his large hands, he could've been a butler. Butlers weren't usually as muscled as him, though.

He was striking with the white beard against ebony skin and bald head. He strode across the room with confidence and placed the tray on the bedside table.

"Good morning," he said in a heavy Edo accent. "I brought your breakfast."

She eyed him and the tray. They'd drugged her at home. She wasn't going to risk being sedated here too.

"What am I doing here?" she asked, crossing arms over her chest as she tried to look past him through the open door.

His massive frame blocked the view. "You are Mr Peters' guest."

"Guest?" She snorted with disdain. "I don't remember accepting an invitation and who the hell is Mr Peters?"

His bullish expression didn't change. "You know him as Osagie."

Her skin prickled at the mention of the man's name. A picture of him in the park, his sharp eyes holding her captive, swam in her mind. She shook her head, wading off the uneasy feeling.

Sweat broke on her forehead, and she paced the floor, rubbing her hand on the back of her neck. She needed to get out of here.

"Look, I'm sure Osagie, Mr Peters, is a nice man and all, but I have to get home. I have a business to run and a paper to research."

"You can't go home. You have to stay in this room, eat your food, and Osagie will come to you when he's ready."

The way he said that made her imagine medieval brides waiting for their new husbands to visit them in their bed chambers. Her spine stiffened, and her anger rose.

She wasn't going to become anyone's fucking "bride" or whatever. She'd divorced one overbearing man. She wouldn't put up with another man's bullshit.

"Didn't you hear me? I don't want to be here." Her body shook, and she sucked in a deep breath. "Look, if you let me go, I won't tell anyone about what's happened. I just want to go home. If this is about money, you can have what's in my account."

The man just shook his head and walked out the door, closing it behind him.

Rushing over, she tried the handle again. Like before it didn't budge. Frustrated, she kicked it, stubbing her big toe.

"Ouch." She hobbled over to the bed and sat on it, rubbing her injured foot. The door was made of metal or something unyielding.

When the pain eased a little, she took the fork from the tray and hid it in the closet. She might need it later as a weapon. Then she showered and got dressed. It'd be better to be fully clothed when she escaped. The expensive clothes in the closet all seemed to be exact fits as if Osagie had stocked them in readiness for her arrival.

Shuddering, she tugged a grey T-shirt over her head and pulled on the dark blue denim trousers. She sat on the bed and slipped her feet into white socks and a pair of leather and suede sneakers.

She could never afford them, but it seemed Osagie was a generous kidnapper. They weren't exactly her trusted, comfortable running shoes, but they were luxurious, and they'd have to do.

The large windows and sparkling cerulean sky gave an illusion of limitless space from the bed. It was just that—a deception. She was caged by the windows and walls and doors. By the entire building.

She hated it.

Tugging at the V-neck of the T-shirt, she sat on the bed. There wasn't much else to do while she waited for Osagie or the other man to return.

Would anyone notice that she wasn't at work today? They would try to contact her but would not raise the alarm unless she didn't show up for a few days. Hopefully, they would reach Mike, and he would tell the authorities.

By then wouldn't it be too late? She was intact for the moment. But she didn't know what Osagie planned for her.

Was he into human trafficking? She'd read horror stories about people who went missing.

Dani was her only close family, and she was abroad right now anyway. So perhaps Gina was a perfect candidate for abduction.

The thought unsettled her more, and her belly knotted.

THREE

OSAGIE STEPPED OUT of the executive car and strode up the short, tiled steps. The sun was low, casting a long shadow across his residence's portico in the Apata Peninsula of Lori Osa.

Nathaniel, the housekeeper, took his briefcase from the back seat and shut the car door with a *thunk*.

Osagie crossed the threshold into the cream-walled foyer. The air-conditioning unit above the entrance blasted cold air onto his face.

"She's all yours," Idehen said as he grabbed his car keys from the narrow table leaning against the wall.

Osagie glanced towards the staircase leading to the next level. "Did she give you a hard time?"

He'd had to go into the office today to deal with some urgent issues, knowing he would have to work from home for the next few days. At least while Georgina was a guest in his home.

He'd left Idehen in charge, the only other person he trusted with her safety.

"Did she hell? Let's just say that I'm glad you're taking over. She hasn't eaten anything all day. I've taken two different meals to her, and she didn't touch any of it. And by the way, she hid a fork in the closet."

Osagie narrowed his eyes. "A fork. Why?"

"So, she can stab you in the back when you're not looking," his friend snort-laughed. "Or hack your balls off. I don't know. All I know is that you should watch your back. She was checking out the exit, trying out the doors. I don't know why you didn't have her locked at the holding facility."

Idehen glanced at his gold wristwatch. "I've really got to go."

"Thanks," Osagie said, dumping his phone and keys on the sideboard.

"No wahala." Idehen walked outside, swapping places with Nathaniel who came in with the black leather laptop bag.

Osagie headed towards the steps and paused. "What are we having for dinner?"

"Owo soup, sir," Nathaniel replied, behind him.

"Good." One of his favourite foods, made with beef, dried fish, large prawns, and spices. "Have it ready in an hour. Set the table for two. I'm going to shower first and then bring our guest down with me."

"Okay, sir. Should I serve the soup with pounded yam or plantain?"

Osagie tilted his head. He was a pounded-yam man. But he suspected Ms Ripped Abs upstairs would prefer the alternative. "Prepare both. Put the briefcase in my office."

"Yes, sir." Nathaniel headed down the corridor.

Osagie walked up the stairs, his footsteps heavy. He'd had a long day and the beginning of a headache.

He walked past Georgina's room without pausing. He wasn't ready for her. He needed to decompress. The shower would help. Home was his haven. When he drove through his gates and stepped through the front door, he wanted to relax and forget his worries.

He had brought work home in the form of Georgina. However, if he treated her like a guest, then she wouldn't be work. Hopefully.

In the master bedroom, he stripped off his clothes and went into the bathroom.

The house was large, more than he needed, considering he lived alone. The staff lived in the annexe.

He'd bought this six-bed two-level house simply to stick his middle finger up at his bigoted, snobbish, former in-laws. Proof that the scrawny homeless Edo boy had become a wealthy Bini tiger of a man and could play in their turf.

His neighbours were the movers and shakers of the political and business classes. People who had made their living off the national cake. They procured nepotistic government appointments and awarded contracts to cabals which were never completed. Thieves, all of them. Yet they looked down their noses at him.

At least he never pretended to be anything else.

Never bamboozled the people with long speeches and promises of change, while filling personal pockets with public funds and bleeding the country dry.

As Osagie dressed in a grey Tee and navy shorts, Idehen's question earlier played on his mind.

Why had he brought Georgina into his home? They had other facilities suitable for holding hostages. Not that he kept hostages frequently.

This kidnapping malarkey was new to him.

He was usually a take-no-prisoner guy.

He'd never captured anyone to detain them for more than a few minutes, maybe a few hours max.

Yet Georgina had been in his home of all places for almost eighteen hours.

For the second time in his adult life, he had a woman who wasn't an employee under his roof—the first time in this house.

Sure, he'd been with many women. In the first ten years after his divorce, he'd fucked his way through the cache of available women, explicitly targeting the well-heeled ones. He'd had a point to prove—formally educated or not, he could get any woman he wanted. When they were in the throes of orgasms, they didn't care about fluent grammar or degree certificates.

When he turned forty, he lost the urge to prove anything and focused on building his businesses.

One was the Arufin Nightclub and subsequently, the Star club where registered, vetted members came for hedonistic, sexual pleasures. Where people could fuck in an environment with set rules, without blurred signals. Where the lines of separation between sex and emotional entanglements were clearly demarcated.

All his erotic encounters were within those walls. He'd never brought a woman home to share his bed.

The only other woman who had lived in his house after his divorce had been Auntie Helen who had been Odigie's nanny.

When his son became old enough, he'd dismissed the woman with a settlement package. The woman now ran a children's home.

That had been in his old house. When Osagie had the massive success with Club Arufin, he bought this one. A home in which he only employed men—Nathaniel and the security team.

Yet, at this moment, there was a woman in his house, in one of the rooms.

Georgina.

After Osagie's encounter with her in the park yesterday morning, and the subsequent decision to detain her until her sister returned from Dubai, he'd made emergency preparations to accommodate her.

There were holding facilities at his warehouse and guest rooms at the club which would have kept her secure. He'd dismissed those options.

Instead, he'd had the windows in one of the bedrooms barricaded, and the door changed to a security one. His assistant had bought new clothes and toiletries and stocked the room.

Despite the short notice, everything had been in place when he'd returned to Highgate Estate last night with Idehen. This time they'd arrived with backup. Two of his team had disabled the security and stood to watch at the security point.

Idehen had driven them to the block with Georgina's apartment and had done his shit with the door. Osagie had never had the patience to learn how to pick locks beyond the basics. But Idehen's subtle skills worked to perfection.

Everything had gone relatively to plan until Georgina had bolted across the room and almost out the front door. Damn, she'd been fast, like a rocket. Luckily, Idehen had caught her in time.

Idehen had carried her, fireman's style to the car and dumped her in the backseat.

Even when they'd arrived at his house, Osagie still hadn't touched her. Idehen had taken her to the room and put her in bed.

Osagie had been avoiding her. He was a disciplined man and always in control.

But the way he'd reacted to Georgina at the park. The fact that he'd thrown caution to the wind and had approached her when he should have kept away had left him a little miffed and pissed off.

He couldn't allow any woman to rattle him.

He had no business being near Georgina beyond finding her sister and getting his money back.

Still, he had to go to her.

Now, she was in his house.

Osagie slid his feet into leather sandals, left his room and walked down the corridor, past a busy, colourful market square mural painted by a famous Nigeria artist. He stopped outside Georgina's room and found the key was in the lock.

He tapped on the door once to warn her someone was coming in and flicked the handle. The slab swung inwards revealing the beige and brown furnished room lit by the setting sun.

Georgina swung her feet to the floor, sitting straight and eyeing him.

The sight of her got his heart racing and his dick hardening.

Her face seemed makeup-free. Maybe mascara and kohl. Her hair tied in a ponytail. She wore skinny jeans and a fitted shirt and sneakers. She'd had her sneakered feet on the bed.

Interesting. Did she intend to sleep in them?

"Hello again, Georgina," Osagie said, keeping his voice soft, unthreatening, perhaps even enticing. He wasn't in the business of scaring women and hoped the gentle approach would appease her.

He just wanted to get through the next few days as calmly as possible until her sister returned.

Metal in the back pocket of her jeans caught the light as she shuffled across the bed. She stood on the other side, arms crossed over chest, plumping her boobs, chin tilted up.

"I can't say the pleasure is mine, Osagie. I don't want to be here," she said, nose wrinkled, lips twisted in disgust.

For the first time since Osagie met the woman, severe displeasure rolled over him. His muscles quivered, and he fought not to grind his teeth in anger.

She might look like any man's wet dream in the body-hugging jeans and V-neck jersey. But the arrogant, scornful expression on her face riled him and reminded him of his former in-laws.

It seemed Georgina had taken one look at him, judged him, and found him wanting. Like he was some filth, she tried to scrap off her shoes.

Okay. He'd taken her by force. So, he deserved her derision, and he was used to being sneered at, all his life.

Yet, this one stung and he couldn't explain it.

If she wanted to be aggressive, he could play the game too. His softly-softly approach didn't seem to be working anyway. It hadn't worked last night either.

If she was bent on casting him as a villain, he would play along.

He stepped across the threshold. "I can say that we are agreed on that point, Ms Badu. I don't want you in my home either."

Her gasp was audible, and her eyes widened. Then her face twisted into a sneer. "Then let me go."

"Oh, I can't do that." He changed the subject, moving onto something less contentious. He didn't like fighting with her. What was the point? "You haven't eaten all day. Tut. Tut. Tut.

As an athlete, you should know the importance of every meal."

She grimaced and averted her gaze, chin dipping.

Sign she knew he was correct. She should've eaten. She didn't have enough body fat for her body to burn. It would start breaking down muscles if she didn't eat soon. And that wasn't good.

"I'm not going to allow you to drug me again," she said in an annoyed voice.

He stopped a few feet away, tilted his head and said in a low voice, trying to sound reassuring. "I won't drug you again as long as you don't try to run again. You can eat dinner with me this evening."

Raising her eyebrows, she offered a questioning gaze. "You mean you're going to let me out of this room?"

"Of course." He took a couple of steps forward.

She did the opposite. Moving away until her back hit the wall and there was nowhere for her to run.

His heart hammered in his chest, and his gut tightened. Not liking her response. Still, he understood it.

"I know you like the outdoors," he continued. "So, in a few days, you'll have all the space and freedom to run again."

She swallowed rapidly, nodding as she bit her bottom lip.

The bright optimism on her face sent warmth through him. The expression was like the one she'd given him in the park.

They stared at each other, and it seemed the world stopped. The steady eye contact made him want to demolish the space between them.

Something happened to him when he was near her. And like yesterday morning, he got sucked into her orbit and seemed to lose himself.

Desire punched his gut. He wanted to touch Georgina, to be caressed in return. Her hands stroking his skin, branding him.

The same need reflected in her sultry gaze. Her pink tongue ran over moist lips, and her throat rippled. Her breathing was choppy.

Heart thumping hard, he leaned in. A few inches closer, and he could taste her sweet lips, caress her smooth skin.

"Sir, the food is ready," Nathaniel's voice came through the open door, breaking the spell.

Georgina stiffened, averting her gaze as if ashamed to be caught this close to him.

"Thank you, Nathaniel. We'll be down shortly." Osagie tilted his head, giving her space. The spell was broken. Just as well.

Whatever was brewing between them shouldn't happen. She was the sweet lady next door. He was ... the opposite of sweet.

Nathaniel's footsteps faded. Georgina still didn't look at him.

"Shall we go and eat?" he asked, breaking the silence.

She turned and looked at him, jaw tightened. "I don't want to be here."

Not this again. He scrubbed a hand over his face and took a deep inhale. "I explained this already."

"I don't care!" she shouted. "Let me go."

His ears rang at the sharp voice, and his headache returned, aggravating him. He didn't need this shit.

"Fine. You want out of here? Here are your choices. Option one, this house where you'll be fed and watered and given the freedom of a houseguest."

She rolled her eyes in response, hands akimbo, chest heaving.

"Option two," he continued, counting off on his fingers. "A cold room in a warehouse. You can sleep on the hard floor. On the upside, your meals will be delivered via mamaput."

She stiffened but said nothing, eyeing him balefully.

"And finally, my favourite option. You chained up in the dungeon of a sex club."

Her mouth dropped open. "A what?"

He suppressed a smile. He'd thrown that in to rile her up and it worked, wiping the self-righteous sneer off her face.

"A sex club. You know what that is, right?"

"Of course, I know what it is."

She glanced behind him. The door stood open, revealing the well-lit hallway.

She was probably calculating how to get out of the house. He expected her to run, but she seemed to hesitate.

Her brown eyes sparkled with cold fire as she glared at him like she wanted to hack his balls off. Was she thinking of doing so with the fork he'd spotted in her back pocket?

He winced. Perhaps he shouldn't have planted that excruciating image in his head.

"What would it be, Ms Badu? Options one, two or three?"

"None of the above."

"Ee-or." He made the sound of a game-show bell. "Wrong answer."

"Is this what you do? Kidnap women for your entertainment?" she demanded.

"No." he skewed his lips and brows as if thinking about it. "Unless she specifically requests an abduction scene."

"Excuse me. No woman wants to be abducted." She stared at him as if he was out of his mind.

"You'd be surprised what people get up to when they let inhibitions go and succumb to their deepest, darkest fantasies. What is your fantasy, Georgina?" He said in a low teasing voice.

He stood close enough to inhale her scent, close enough to see her chest heave as she inhaled sharply, close enough to watch the pulse thumping on her collar.

She seemed flustered for a few seconds before she recovered. "Well, I don't like being abducted and kept locked in a room by a stranger, you bastard."

The metal of the fork flashed in her hand, and she lunged at him.

One of the good things about sparring with Idehen was that Osagie had learnt to avoid being hit. Idehen's punches were powerful and had knocked many men out. So, avoiding them was an excellent way of preventing concussions.

He saw the blow coming from Georgina and dodged it, grabbed her arm, disarming her. The cutlery clattered onto the floor.

She didn't seem fazed by it, though. She twisted to the side, lifted her knee in a half-side kick and planted it in his groin.

Fuck. Pain exploded through him. He grunted, doubling over, and collapsing.

Footsteps pounded on the tiled floor as she ran out of the room.

He stayed on the floor, coughing, and gulping in air until the severe agony eased.

Now, he was furious.

The woman didn't want to stay in his house? Fine. He wouldn't force her to stay. The men would take her to the warehouse. Then he could have his home back and his peace of mind too.

He took his time getting off the floor. No need to hurry or go after her.

Georgina couldn't go far. If she managed to leave the house, there were security men on the grounds and by the gates. The perimeter walls were too high to climb, and there were broken glass and razor wires at the top.

Osagie pulled himself up to his feet, straightened and left the room. As he went downstairs, the sound of barking dogs became insistent.

The guards usually released his two Alsatians, Bruno and Benn, at dusk each day. It sounded like they were loose already.

He walked across the downstairs hall to check the living room for Georgina when he heard a loud shriek.

Nope. She wasn't in the living room. She was outside, and it seemed, she'd met the dogs.

Oh, well. She could stay out there and get acquainted with the guards and dogs while he had his dinner. The owo soup was getting cold. He hadn't eaten since breakfast.

He turned towards the dining room.

"Osagie, help me!" Georgina shouted in a hoarse voice. She sounded terrified.

Shit. The guards couldn't have hurt her. They were under strict instructions to handle with care.

He swivelled and raced to the partially ajar front door, yanking it fully open. He jumped on to the portico and exhaled in relief.

Georgina stood halfway between the porch and the gates, frozen to the spot, eyes squeezed shut.

The unshackled dogs were about two feet from her, teeth bared, making low snarling sounds. Two guards stood behind Bruno and Benn.

Georgina must have been running when they chased her. One of the guards would have used a whistle to halt the animals. Otherwise, they would have taken her down.

He strode towards them, his sandals crunching on the pebbles.

Georgina must have heard his approach. Her eyes flicked open wildly. "Send the dogs away."

He was stunned.

She was frightened of the dogs?

He'd always thought she was a fearless woman. He remembered her from her glory days on the track as the African and Commonwealth 400m champion. He'd believed she would've become an Olympic gold medallist.

That daring woman couldn't be afraid of dogs?

But he saw it in her full body tremors and harried expression.

His chest tightened, and he rubbed a hand over it. He didn't like seeing her frightened.

Yet, she'd fucking kicked him in the nuts. He was still sore. And she was adamant about not wanting to stay in his house. So, he should arrange for her to be taken to the warehouse.

"Why should I? You kicked me in the balls," he said, although there wasn't much heat in his tone.

"I had good reason," she snapped, her fury overriding her anxiety. "You kidnapped me. Don't be a fucking asshole as well."

His couldn't help the quick bark of laughter.

Her directness caught him by surprise. He killed the laughter and watched her.

She had an odd mix of defiance and pleading in her face, which melted his heart and soothed his anger. He sighed in resignation.

"The dogs won't bite you," he offered in the way of soothing her. Bruno and Benn wouldn't move unless they were commanded.

"Please, make them go away," she said, sounding reedy. Her breathing was still choppy.

"Take the dogs," Osagie ordered.

The men came forward and attached the dog collars.

As soon as the dogs were on leads, Gina ran to Osagie and launched herself at him. Her arms wrapped around his neck in a death grip.

"Th—tha—nk—you." Her body trembled, her teeth chattered, and her legs gave way.

She buried her face against his neck. The next second she was crying.

Not pretend crying. Not sniffling. This was full-on sobbing. Getting his shirt wet kind of weeping.

For a moment, Osagie froze.

He didn't do crying women. The crocodile tears of his ex-wife were enough to last him a lifetime. Tears had zero effect on him. Women didn't bother to try it with him. He didn't even do cuddles after sex.

Yet, instead of untangling himself from Georgina, he scooped her legs up into his arms. "I've got you."

She clung tight and wept hard.

He listened to her cry as he carried her indoors. He should take her back upstairs to her room so she could cry to her heart's content.

He didn't.

He went into the living room, settling on a sofa with her on his lap.

Although her body was firm in places, she was all woman, soft and fragrant, petite and perfect in his embrace.

Guilt pelted his skin with heat because he had been the cause of her distress. He hadn't intended to do this to her—to take her or bring her to his home.

His actions just underlined how bad a person he was, how unsuitable he was for her.

"I'm sorry. I won't let the dogs hurt you. You're safe," Osagie said in a soothing tone, rubbing his palm on her back in circles.

For the first time in twenty years, he felt like the asshole she'd accused him of, and he didn't like the feeling.

FOUR

GINA DIDN'T KNOW how long she stayed on Osagie's lap.

He didn't seem in a hurry to get rid of her. Yet he didn't do more than whisper calming words and rub her back soothingly.

The comfort he provided was something she hadn't received in a long time.

Everyone looked at her and saw a strong, capable woman. She was expected to take care of others. Of her mother when she'd been sick, her sister whenever she got into trouble, and her employees because she was a boss.

Since her mother died, she hadn't grieved properly, not really.

As the first daughter, all the responsibility of settling her parents' estate had fallen on her shoulders.

Dani, on her part, had become a party animal. Gina assumed that was her way of coping with their mother's loss. The same way Gina has taken to working so hard she came home exhausted every night.

So, she hadn't been this vulnerable since her mother's cancer diagnosis. Hadn't allowed herself to breakdown, and certainly not in front of another person.

Somehow, she didn't feel the need to put on her superwoman cloak right now. The sight of those dogs triggered her to the point, she didn't care.

However, what surprised her more was that Osagie was allowing her to cry on his lap. A man who had abducted her. He hadn't dragged her back to the room and locked her away. Especially since she'd kneed his groin.

Even Mike had never held her like this.

And Osagie wasn't Mike.

What was wrong with her? She had a man, even if he was more a business-partner-with-benefits rather a steady boyfriend.

Mike wasn't ready to settle down. She wasn't looking for a husband. They had an understanding that worked for them. They could see other people too.

Osagie didn't seem the kind of man who would settle for FWB relationships.

His intensity was overwhelming.

When he'd walked into the room earlier, her breath had caught, her heart thumping against her chest.

Without the hooded outfit, he was stunning. A dark angel. His hair was white on his scalp and around his chin, softening the perfect hardness of his face. His gaze settled on her and his sensuous lips curved into a half-smile.

The soft, panty-melting way he said her name made tingles travel down her spine. Her clit pulsed. Her mouth dried out as she watched him stride across the room like a tiger stalking deer.

When he neared her, and she breathed his smell of soap and clean man, she nearly succumbed to the need to bridge the gap between them and kiss him. She imagined tearing his clothes off, pushing him onto the bed and riding the sexual energy oozing off him until they were both sated and exhausted.

Only the voice of someone mentioning food saved her.

She'd known then she had to get away from Osagie. How could she be attracted to a man who had kidnapped her? A man who was keeping her captive. Sure, he'd mentioned letting her go in a few days. What if that was a lie? What if his intent was worse?

Adrenaline flushed through her. Without thinking, she tried stabbing him with the fork, but he evaded the jab. She recovered quickly, kneed his groin, feigned to the right to distract him, and ran across the room.

She heard his curse behind her, but she didn't stop as she ran into the hallway, her heart pounding loud and fast it could've punched a hole in her chest.

She reached the top of the stairs, and with two more strides, she jumped down the steps. At the bottom, she chanced a glance backwards. Seeing no one, she glanced around and ducked under an archway before heading towards what she hoped was the exit.

Please be unlocked, she prayed as she reached for the solid wooden door's handle and yanked. Surprisingly, it gave in, making her stumble.

Another backwards glance and still no Osagie or his servant.

She must have disabled him with her kick to the groin. Anyway, it was more important to get out and then she would find help somehow.

She rushed out onto the portico held up by white columns, down the short stairs onto a gravel driveway. A carport stood to her right. Black gates loomed to the left, about one hundred and fifty metres.

She ran towards it, hoping it would also be easy to open the gates, the stones crunching beneath the sneakers.

As she reached the edge of the house, movement caught the corner of her eyes.

At first, she thought it was a guard and increased her speed. Then she heard barking and turned.

Two freaking giant Alsatians as big as horses were bounding in her direction.

Terrified, she froze, body trembling, heart thumping, breath choppy. Dark spots flitted through her eyes, spreading as her panic increased.

The dogs were on her now. They were going to bite her, eat her alive.

She opened her mouth and screamed.

Suddenly the dogs stopped as if by remote control, both at the same time. They bared their teeth and growled as if she was their dinner.

Close to hyperventilating and blacking out, she kept still and upright. If she moved, the dogs would be on her.

As a nine-year-old walking home from school one day, she'd been chased and bitten by a neighbour's dog. She'd been hospitalised. Her father had been furious, he'd sued the dog owners. The dog had been put down, but it hadn't been enough for him. Eventually, he dropped the charges when others interceded for the family.

The event had traumatised Gina so much, she wouldn't knowingly visit anyone with dogs. She ran in her local park at dawn before the dog walkers came out. As soon as she saw a dog, leashed or not, she went home.

"Can I get you something to drink? Water?" Osagie's quiet voice vibrated through her, pulling her from her thoughts.

Her cheeks heated. She'd stopped bawling like a baby and hadn't moved from his lap. She wriggled to get up, and he let her go.

She looked away, unable to meet his gaze. How could she look him in the eyes when she'd let him carry her, let him soothe her tears? "I need to use the toilet."

"There's one on the other side of the foyer," he said calmly.

She hesitated, remembering the dogs. Did they come into the house?

"The dogs are outside." He seemed to read her mind.

She nodded and rushed out. In the bathroom, she turned the lock on the door and looked at herself in the mirror.

There were tear streaks on her oval face, and her mocha-hued skin looked sallow.

What had she been thinking, running into Osagie's arms?

Granted at the time she'd been caught between the devil and the deep blue sea.

At least she'd been able to catch Osagie unawares. She had no defence against dogs.

Osagie had been kind, lifting her when she would have fallen. Was it possible the kidnapper had a heart? Could she convince him to let her go?

There was only one way to find out.

She splashed cold water on her face and dried it with a towel. Brushing down the top of her hair, she re-tightened the ponytail band and cleaned out the smudged mascara with a damp tissue.

When she came out of the bathroom, Osagie stood by the living room door.

She narrowed her eyes, and her muscles stiffened.

Did he think she would try to run again?

"Are you okay?" he asked, his midnight eyes piercing. He sounded concerned.

She puffed out a breath. "I'm fine. Someone mentioned something about food earlier. I'm hungry."

There was no point starving herself. It seemed she wouldn't be getting out of here soon, anyway. Not with those dogs outside. She had to figure out a way to bypass them.

A small smile tugged the corner of his lips. "Sure. This way." He led them to the dining room. Magnolia walls, dark wooden table, matching padded leather chairs. Only two places were set with placemats, tumblers, and cutlery.

As if on cue, a young man walked in. He wore a black apron over jeans and T-shirt and carried a large tray. He set steaming bowls of soup down for each of them. Then he lowered a plate of pounded yam in front of Osagie.

"Madam, would you like pounded yam or plantain with your soup?" He sounded like the Nathaniel from earlier.

"Plantain, please," Gina replied. The food smelled delicious, and her mouth watered.

The servant lowered the plate of steamed plantain onto the placemat. He opened the fridge in the corner and took out a water bottle, placing it on the table. Then he popped out and returned with a bowl of water.

Osagie washed his hands before the server left them alone.

"I prefer eating with my hands. Do you mind?" Osagie's inscrutable expression made her uneasy.

"Why should I?" she said defensively.

"Some people think it's barbaric to eat with your fingers," he said.

"Those people are idiots," she replied.

His eyes warmed, and his face relaxed as if she'd passed a test.

She lifted the fork and cut a chunk of plantain before dipping it into the bowl of soup. When she placed it on her tongue, the flavours of spice and smoky fish filled her mouth.

"Mmmm." She chewed, savouring the food. The combination of the sweet plantain and spicy soup was bliss. "This is wonderful."

"I'm glad you like it. It's one of my favourite meals, although, after a long day, the smoothness of the yam is more comforting." Osagie lifted the plate. "Here try a bite and see what I mean."

She looked up, and her heart stuttered.

He was offering her food from his plate, an intimate act, something done by lovers.

Get a grip, Gina. You're his captive.

Maybe he got a kick out of playing house with his captives.

"No. Don't worry. I'm okay with this."

"Go on. Just a little piece. I want to know what you think about the yam compared to the plantain."

He looked at her as if they were lovers, and he considered her opinion important. The fluttering in her chest returned.

He wasn't asking her to do anything terrible.

"Okay." She reached across with her fork and scraped a little piece, then dipped it in her bowl.

He watched her intently as she scooped it into her mouth and swallowed.

"And?" he asked expectantly.

"And it's great. The yam amplifies the soup flavours. It's not worse or better. Simply different."

He nodded and returned to his meal, using his fingers to cut, dip and scoop. He ate with gusto, his enjoyment evident as his throat rippled and his lips smacked.

How could someone eating be so erotic?

He lifted his head, and she looked down quickly, cheeks heating, hoping he hadn't caught her staring.

"I guessed you would prefer the plantain and I was correct," he said after they'd eaten for a while, sounding amused.

She shrugged. "Well, plantain is healthier than yam."

He chuckled. "I knew you would say that."

"What? You read minds now?"

"No. Just an educated guess. A skill I acquired a long time ago, being able to predict people and situations. But I admit I didn't predict your fear of dogs."

"And you didn't guess my knee in your groin either."

He chuckled, shaking his head. "You've got me there."

His laughter was a warm rumble that vibrated through her chest. He was gorgeous, no doubt about it. And she could sit here and listen to his voice all day.

Great meal. Great company.

She enjoyed his presence when he was chatting and laughing. He seemed like a reasonable human being when he wasn't invading people's homes and abducting them.

Bringing her back to why?

"Why am I really here?" She put her cutlery on the empty plate.

He looked up while washing his hands. He'd finished his meal too.

"I can't tell you that. Not yet." He raised his hand when she opened her mouth to protest. "But I'm going to promise you that I won't drug you again or set the dogs on you or do anything to hurt you. In return, you will stay here for the next few days until I'm ready to let you go home."

"When will that be, though?" This whole situation made no sense to her. "Is this about money? Do you want a ransom?"

Kidnappings for ransom was rife in the country. Perhaps that was how he made money, stealing people, and forcing their loved ones to pay for their releases.

Her stomach knotted that she'd allowed a man with such intentions to comfort her. That she'd sat at the table and eaten a meal with him like they were friends.

"Yes and no."

"I don't understand."

He puffed out a breath. "Yes, you're here because of money, but I don't want a ransom from you. Not yet at least."

What did that mean?

"Look, I don't have a lot of money. But if that's what you want, I can transfer whatever is in my account into yours, right now—"

"I told you I don't want your money."

"What then? I can't sit here. I have a business to run. People will be worried about me."

"Quite." He leaned forward and withdrew a phone from his back pocket. "That's why you're allowed one phone call."

It sounded like a prison, although she hadn't figured out what her crime was.

He pushed the phone across the table.

Her eyes widened as she picked it. "It's my phone. How did you get it?"

"We took it from your apartment, along with your laptop and other items. They will all be returned to you once this is over."

"And when will this be over?" She made air-quotes with her fingers, her annoyance rising.

"Hopefully soon and you can return to your life. In the meantime, make the call. Tell whoever it is that you're out of town for a few days."

She stared at the fully charged phone in her hand. He must have brought her charger along too.

The screen lock was on, thankfully. So Osagie or whoever hadn't been able to access her contacts and other details.

She lifted her gaze to meet his. "I can call anyone I want?"

"Yes. You are welcome to contact a friend or family or employee. Tell them you're okay and are away from home for a few days. However, you should not contact the police. We know where you live and where you work and your loved ones."

He let the threat hang in the air, and it chilled her bones.

No matter how congenial this man had been towards her, he was still a dangerous man. She couldn't allow herself to forget that.

Her heart raced, and her hand trembled. It took a few deep breaths before she could stop the shaking and unlock her phone.

Who could she call in this situation?

Dani was out of the country, and Mike was unreachable. She had close friends she could contact. But did she want to get people worried?

What if it was a ruse for Osagie to find out who they would call for a ransom demand? She didn't want to get anyone else entangled in this.

She couldn't involve the police anyway.

Aside from the abduction, Osagie hadn't done anything excessive yet. Best not to provoke him. She would bide her time until the opportunity presented to escape.

The only thing left was the gym. She had to close it.

She lifted her head. Osagie watched her as if he was trying to figure out what she would do.

"I have to close the gym until further notice. I'm not there, and Mike is not there."

"Who is Mike?" His tone was sharp, and his jaw tightened.

"Mike is my business partner."

"And your lover?" His mouth thinned, his chin poking forward. Was he jealous?

Her cheeks heated at the intimate question. "No."

It wasn't a lie. Lover implied love or being in love.

She wasn't in love with Mike. He was a friend-with-benefits. The first time they'd gotten together, she'd been feeling low after her mother's cancer diagnosis. He'd comforted her, and they'd ended up in bed together. The next day they'd talked and agreed it was nothing more than sex. They'd been together a few times since. But it stayed physical only. Life carried on until the next time they both felt the need to scratch the itch.

Her marriage and her ex had drained her, mentally. She hadn't been emotionally ready to get involved with another man.

Are you ready to get involved now? With Osagie?

Hell, no! Where the hell did the question come from?

Osagie was a dangerous man. No decent human being would kidnap a woman. Or keep her locked in his house.

Never mind that he'd saved her from the scary dogs. That he'd scooped her into his arms, soothed and apologised to her. He'd sounded sincere too.

Every time he smiled, her body tightened with need. She should hate how damned sexy he was.

How could someone as brutal as he was, also be so freaking sexy and normal?

Seriously, she'd sat here and had dinner with her kidnapper like it was the most normal thing in the world. Like she was really his house guest.

Who did that?

Gina Badu and Osagie Peters, apparently.

What was going on with her? She'd met and dated some sexy men in her time—great sports personalities, famous musicians, and film stars. So, she shouldn't be so infatuated with Osagie. At forty, she'd been around the block and could separate boys from men.

And Osagie was all man—

"Georgina?" Osagie's voice rumbled.

She blinked rapidly and frowned. "Yes?"

"You were going to make a phone call?" he waved at the phone in her hand.

She'd been swept away, thinking of him, she'd forgotten what she should be doing.

"Right. Phone call." She fumbled with the gadget to hide her embarrassment. "I'm going to call and ask the staff to close the gym until after Christmas. I will also need to send an email to all our members to notify them of the closure. I'm going to need my laptop as well. Is that okay?"

He narrowed his eyes and wrinkled his brow. "No laptop. Tell the staff to send the email."

"I can't. The only two people with the account details are Mike and me. If I ask Mike to do it, he'll ask questions. I thought you didn't want unnecessary scrutiny." She spread her open palms as she leaned back in the chair.

"Fine. You can have your laptop. Only briefly and for the email."

"Yes!" She did a fist pump. This was a big win. With a phone and a laptop, anything was possible.

***

Two days later, Gina's phone pinged with a message. She grabbed the phone and saw the sender.

Her sister.

Heart racing, she looked in Osagie's direction.

Osagie sat at the solid oak desk in his home office.

She was on the brown leather sofa with her laptop on the low wooden table. She could use it for university work and respond to urgent emails.

He only allowed her to use her phone in his presence and took the gadgets away overnight.

His face was focused in concentration on whatever he was doing on the computer, his fingers tapping away on the keyboard.

Soul music played in the background from small yet powerful Wi-Fi speakers mounted on the walls' corners. Osagie loved R'n'B, which was something they had in common. Surprisingly.

She hadn't left the house since her arrival.

Yet there were worse things that spending time in Osagie's company.

The man was freaking hot.

Today, a dove-grey shirt stretched across his broad shoulders and solid chest. The long sleeves rolled up to his elbows, showing muscular tattooed arms. He had the most compelling warm cobalt eyes which tended to turn to cold granite when he was angry.

Not to mention the perfectly chiselled jawline covered in the salt and pepper beard or the gorgeous lips she desperately wanted to taste.

When he was in the same room, she spent the time sneaking glances at him when he wasn't looking. And she'd had sexy dreams about him.

Ridiculous.

But Osagie Peters had invaded her life both real and imaginary. Physically and mentally.

Her phone buzzed again.

Damn. She needed to get a grip. She was a hostage, not on a weekend vacation or something.

She huffed out a sigh and opened the messages.

Hey, sis. Just wanted to tell you that my flight back is scheduled for tomorrow morning. I should be home by tomorrow night.

Good. Her sister was coming home early. Gina typed out a response.

That's great. I'm not—

"Georgina?" Osagie's sexy voice carried a warning.

Her cheeks heated like he'd caught her doing something naughty.

"Yes, Mr Peters." She pretended she didn't know why he was calling her out and looked in his direction.

His dark, piercing gaze was on her. "You know you're not allowed to use your phone."

She swallowed. "I'm allowed to use it in your presence. I'm in your presence now, aren't I?"

Raising his brow, he swivelled his black leather armchair and stood. "Do you really want to try my patience?"

"How? It's only a message from my sister."

He came around and stopped the other side of the coffee table. "Let me see."

"Don't you trust me?" she asked with a frown as she handed the phone over.

"I trust you as much as you trust me."

"Fair enough."

He shrugged and swiped through her messages. Luckily, there wasn't anything incriminating, or she would be worried. He handed the phone back to her and turned towards the desk.

"Why am I really here?" Gina asked. "I don't know any kidnapper who would keep their captive in a mansion, feed her and let her work online. You haven't demanded any ransom that I know of, not that I have anyone who can pay it, anyway. And you haven't demanded sex."

He treated her like a guest rather than a prisoner. Well, a visitor who couldn't leave the house.

"Do you want to have sex with me?" His eyes sparkled, his lips curving into a smirk.

He had been easy-going since the incident with the dogs. He'd been here every day, and they shared this office space. While he worked, she worked. They ate dinner together and had discussed politics and the country's economy.

But he was yet to reveal the reason she was here.

"I..." she spluttered and lifted the glass of water to her lips to cool her heated body. She'd opened that door, and he hadn't hesitated about walking straight through it. "That's not what I mean."

"But would you, though?" his tone intensified, making her core clench and her nipples hardened.

He shoved his hands into the pockets, which drew her attention to the bulge, tenting his perfectly tailored pinstriped charcoal trousers.

Damn, that was quite a package. One she wished to unwrap and use for pleasure.

There was no denying there was something between them.

Attraction.

Since the first day she'd had a panic attack because of the dogs, she hadn't had any urges to run or get away from him.

Instead, she'd looked forward to their daily interactions.

Despite the danger he exuded sometimes, there was a quiet reassurance about him, a comforting calmness.

He wasn't the most talkative man in the world. There were things about him she wanted to find out.

Like why did he live in this vast house alone? Did he have a wife? Children?

What was his plan for her?

Did he intend to kill her?

Yet if he intended to kill her, why keep her alive?

Why leave her untouched?

Maybe he wasn't attracted to her.

But desire burned in his gaze when he looked at her?

The man was cold and calculating, looked like a GQ cover model, and built like a rugby fly-half. He was rich, ruthless, and powerful.

Yet absolutely freaking gorgeous and the most tempting man she'd ever encountered.

"There's no point asking me because it's not going to happen. You're not into me."

Not that she didn't think she was beautiful. Beauty was in the eye of the beholder.

He gave an unbelieving bark of laughter. "Are you kidding me? From the first day, I saw you, I wanted you. I've pictured your muscular thighs gripping my shoulders tight while I'm licking your pussy. I've wondered if you taste as sweet as you look."

O.M.G! Talk about shooting your shot.

She was ready to combust and clamped her mouth shut to prevent the moan bubbling in her throat. Already wet, her core clenched. Her skin heated, and her nipples became sensitive.

The image he painted filled her mind. She closed her eyes, tilting her head back. She wanted to spread her legs and invite him over to make the fantasy a reality.

"I've imagined doing so many things to you, Georgina. From my recollections, though, you made it quite clear you didn't like me. I don't force women into my bed. I don't need to." His tone was sarcastic and cold. Her eyes popped open as he pulled a phone out of his pocket and tapped the screen. "There were over twenty people in my Star app queue."

A twinge bloomed in her chest. She'd already figured a man as sexy as Osagie wouldn't lack female company. But... "What is Star app? Is that a dating app?"

His eyes narrowed as he settled on the opposite sofa. "Similar. But it's designed exclusively for Arufin VIP members, who use it to book partners and sessions at the Star Club. Each member goes through a screening process for security and health purposes, which involves regular STD tests. The HIV status is listed on their profile."

"Hang on. You own a sex club?" Her brows jumped almost to her hairline. He'd mentioned chaining her to a dungeon in a sex club. Now it all clicked into place.

"Yes. And a night club in the adjacent building. And other businesses. Have you ever been to a sex club?"

"Hell, no!" She reared back. "I can't even remember the last time I was in a nightclub. It's been a few years."

"Good. You should keep it that way." He shifted as he tried to get up.

"What do you mean 'keep it that way'?" she asked, suddenly irritated. Was he mocking her?

"I mean a good woman like you should keep away from nightclubs and sex clubs. In fact, you should never visit Arufin."

That 'good woman' label just wound her up even more. It implied she hadn't lived because she'd never done anything depraved.

"How come I should keep away from there and yet you own those venues?"

"We're two different kinds of people?"

"How? Don't tell me it's because you're a man and I'm a woman."

"No. It's because I'm bad and you're good. Think of it this way. I'm the big bad wolf, Arufin is the evil forest, and you are Little Red. If you ever step foot into Arufin, I will devour you."

His gaze was intense, eating her up on the spot.

She broke eye contact, running her fingers over the mousepad to wake the sleeping laptop.

The man had just threatened her. Yet heat pooled low in her belly as she pictured him devouring her in different raunchy positions.

Her face and body burned, and her core clenched.

"Ehm." She coughed to clear her throat. "If you'll excuse me, I have a paper to research."

He didn't say anything for a few seconds. She felt the heat of his gaze on her skin but refused to look at him.

If she looked at him, then she would wonder about his sex club and imagine the two of them tangled up.

She grabbed the printed paper on top of the broadsheets he'd been reading yesterday as a distraction. It was a festively decorated flyer for 'Father Christmas's visit to the Itohan Peters Children's Home.'

"What's this?" she asked, waving the flyer.

"It's nothing for you to worry about." He extended his hand, and she placed the flyer into his palm.

"Are you thinking of going to the event?" she teased.

He shrugged, looking away as if he was embarrassed.

"Well, you've done some bad things. So, I think you're on the naughty list."

"I've been on the naughty list a long time."

The way he said that made her heart race. But something else crept into her mind. "Unless you are Father Christmas himself."

He didn't meet her gaze and picked up a newspaper.

"Oh, my goodness! You are the Father Christmas. Of course." She slapped her cheeks with her hands. She pictured him in a tailored red suit with white fur collar, cuffs, and front pockets.

He was going to visit a children's home as Santa. So sweet and so damned sexy too. Wow.

Her heart squeezed tight, and butterflies fluttered in her belly.

Without thinking, she shoved papers off the coffee table and sat in front of Osagie. "I want to see you in the Santa suit."

"Not happening." Frowning, he lifted the newspaper, blocking her out of his view.

"Please, Santa," she said in a sultry voice and lowered hands onto his thighs. "I've been good all year. I'll do anything to see you dressed as Santa."

A fantasy created in her mind the morning she saw him in the park. She'd imagined sitting on his lap and riding his dick while he was dressed in the red suit.

Muscles tightening, he dropped the broadsheet on the side table.

"You really want me dressed in a red suit?" he asked after staring at her with an inscrutable expression for a few seconds.

"Yes." She bobbed her head, getting excited.

"You'll see me in a Santa suit on Christmas Day. But in return, I want something from you." He lifted her left hand, trailing his thumb over her palm.

Tingles travelled down her arm. Her clit pulsed, her nipples hardening as her heart raced. Damn, she was putty in Osagie's hands, and she didn't mind at all.

She swallowed, working saliva into her dry mouth. "What?"

"I've been invited to a New Year's Eve party, and I'd like you to be my escort for the event."

She blinked several times and glanced at him incredulously. "Me. Your escort? You're going to allow me out of this house?"

"Of course. You're not going to be here on New Year's Eve. I told you I'd let you go in a few days. Don't you believe me?" He sounded annoyed and dropped her hand, looking affronted.

"No. I'm sorry." She shook her head. "I forgot about that. Why me, though? You have numerous women on your app waiting list."

Was she really getting green-eyed? Did she care if he had a harem of women? She wasn't ready to get emotionally attached, remember?

"If I wanted any of them, they wouldn't be on a waiting list. But I understand if you have other plans." He reached for the newspaper.

"No." She placed her hand on his arm, stopping him. "I don't have anything else planned."

He retook her hand, threading his callused fingers between hers.

The fluttering feeling returned in her belly.

"So, Georgina, will you be my New Year's Eve date?" His lips curved in a beautiful smile, fire back in his gorgeous eyes.

Take that, waiting list! She did a mental fist-pump as she grinned. "Yes, Mr Peters. I'll be your escort. On one condition."

He arched one dark brow, arms spread. "Other than me in a Santa suit?"

"Yes. Can I go to the mall? I'd like to pick up some items before Christmas. And shop for the party dress too."

"Done."

"Just like that?"

"Sure. There's a new mall not far from here."

"Great. And another thing. You'll let me decorate this place. It looks miserable in here, and Christmas is two days away."

Osagie's face brightened as if she'd just granted a wish and he chuckled. "Of course, whatever you want."

FIVE

THE NEXT MORNING, Gina got out of bed with a flutter of excitement in her belly. The sky was still grey, and the sun wasn't fully up. She was an early riser.

She'd been in Osagie's house for five days and for the first time she would leave the house today. She would be in a crowd of shoppers, see other humans aside from Osagie and his team.

She grabbed the long silk robe matching the negligee she'd slept in and wrapped it around her body. One of the perks of living in Osagie's house. Everything he'd given her was luxurious.

The plan was to get some water to drink and run on the treadmill. Then shower and dress before tea and breakfast. Afterwards, shopping. Yay.

Osagie woke later because he usually stayed late at the nightclub. The last two mornings he'd risen early and joined her in the small gym next to his office. He used the free weights and punching bag while she used the running machine and the yoga mat.

Although she missed having the wind on her face as she ran, his company made up for the inconvenience.

With bouncing steps, she hurried out of the bedroom, across the hallway and down the stairs. The lights were on, which meant Nathaniel was up. He was an early riser too.

"I should be back by then. I'll speak to you later." Osagie's voice came from the living room. Sounded like he was alone, perhaps talking on the phone.

Was he working already?

She entered the living room, and her stomach dropped.

Osagie was dressed in pinstripe navy trousers, white dress shirt, dark tie, and polished black leather brogues. The suit jacket hung across the back of an armchair.

He'd never been this fully clothed at this hour.

Noticing her at the threshold, he pushed off the cream leather settee. "Good morning, Georgina. How are you?"

"Morning. Are you going somewhere?" She frowned as her chest tightened.

"Yes, I have a flight to catch this morning." He strode towards her, phone in hand.

Her breath hitched. "Flight? You're going away?"

He reached her and tucked the gadget into his trouser back pocket. "Just for a few hours. I'll be back tonight."

"Oh." Her stomach clenched, and her chest tightened. She should've known not to trust his promise of letting her out of the house. Shoulders drooped, she swivelled to leave. "Have a nice trip."

Before she could cross the threshold, a hand landed on her shoulder. "Wait. You don't look okay. What's wrong?"

"It's nothing." She tried to shrug his hand away.

His touch signified concern and comfort, which was deceptive. Osagie couldn't be concerned. He was a ruthless man who cared for only himself.

He came around to stand in front of her, palms cupping her shoulders, body tilted so he could see her face. "It's something. Tell me."

His cologne perfumed the air—something warm and zesty. His curious dark eyes bore into her, eyebrows drawn together.

She puffed out a heavy breath. "Fine. I thought you said we were going shopping today. I understand if you changed your mind."

"No. I didn't change my mind."

"But you're going on a trip—"

"And you're going shopping." He slipped into the room. She turned as he took a wallet out of his jacket, opened it, and pulled out a black card. "This is for you. Get whatever you need."

She eyed the card in his hand and looked up at him. "You're serious. I can go to the mall?"

"Of course. Unless you've changed your mind."

"Of course not." Warmth blooming in her chest, she grabbed the card, and her fingers grazed his.

Tingles shot up her arm. Their gazes locked, and her heart skipped a beat.

"Good." He smiled, his thumb grazing the back of her hand. "Idehen is coming over later to take you."

"Okay." She twirled the card between her fingers. "And the pin code?"

He pulled out a piece of paper. "Here."

"Thank you." She could afford to buy her own clothes. But she was here because of him, and she was doing him a favour by attending the party. So, it was his expense, fair and square.

He stepped into her personal space and took a deep breath, eyes burning into her. His jaw clenched and rippled. The intensity of his gaze made her heart skip another beat. It looked like he was fighting to hold something in, something threatening to explode.

"I'm sorry I can't go with you. Are you going to miss me?"

Shrugging, she didn't say anything. What could she say?

She would miss him. He'd become an unexpected part of her daily life these past five days. Not spending the day with him would be weird.

But she couldn't say any of that.

He was the man who took her from her home and kept her away from her life.

"I'm going to miss you," he whispered in a thick voice. "The day won't be the same without you."

Heat pulsed through her. The rest of the world blurred away, and they seemed to be the only two people in it.

"Why?" she asked and swallowed thickly, her tongue darting out to wet her lips.

He lowered a hand to her hip while the other cupped her nape, bringing their bodies flushed together.

"Because you're smart and beautiful and funny. You captivated me from the moment I saw you. Made me crave you. You woke a part of me that was dead for many years."

Eyes widening, her jaw dropped. Talk about a surprise.

Her world flipped on its axis, and before she could think better of it, she did the most natural thing that came to mind.

She rose onto tiptoes and pressed her lips against his sensuous mouth.

His arms circled her. A growl rumbled in this throat. He returned her kiss, palm cupping her cheek while the other held her hip.

She lost herself in him. In the kiss.

All the days of craving him. Finally, she tasted him.

His lips were perfect, not too hard, and not too soft. He groaned and cradled her into his body. His touch was tender yet possessive. Like she was precious. Like he couldn't get enough of her.

Osagie was a kissing god. The world spun. Her toes curled, and her pulse skipped. He held her like she belonged to him, setting fire to her core.

There was only the flimsy silk robe and negligee separating his hand from her skin. She wanted him to touch her, to fulfil the fantasies she'd had about him.

Growling, he lifted his head only a few inches. His eyes burned with passion.

"Sweetheart, I don't want to leave. But the flight..." his voice rumbled.

The endearment caught her off guard. Did he really care, or was it just sex-talk?

She nodded and swallowed the lump in her throat. "I understand. I'll see you tonight?"

"Sure. And I look forward to coming home so I can spread you out on my bed and taste every part of you until you scream and forget everything else."

A moan escaped her lips as her core clenched, and her panties dampened. "Mr Peters, you may have to miss that flight."

She grabbed his head, leaned in, and kissed him hard before breaking it off. "But you're going to make it up to me, for driving me crazy with anticipation until your return."

He chuckled. "I'll be happy to make it up to you. I have a few surprises for you."

"In that case, I look forward to them." She giggled as he kissed the corner of her mouth briefly.

"Nathaniel is out on an errand. Are you okay with sorting your breakfast? The kitchen is stocked." He grabbed his jacket.

"Yeah. No worries. I'll sort it." She moved aside for him to stride past.

He took the brown leather briefcase on the table in the foyer, opened the front door and turned to her. "See you later, sweetheart."

Her heart lurched. At this moment, he looked like her dream man on his way to a business trip.

She was excited about seeing him tonight. "Later, Mr Peters. Have a safe flight."

He had a gorgeous smile on his face as he stepped onto the portico and strode to the car, the back door held by one of the security men. Osagie said something she couldn't hear to the man before sliding into the back seat.

She waved at him as the door clunked shut. Then the car rolled towards the gates already opened. A few seconds later, it disappeared past the barrier.

With a sigh, she shut the front door and leaned against it. The card in her hand caught her gaze, and a smile bloomed on her face.

Osagie had kissed her.

She traced index fingers over her lips. The kiss had been sweet and intense.

He'd promised to take it a step further tonight.

Okay. The whole situation was still strange. This was not conventional dating.

But he cared about her. She'd seen it in his eyes, in the way he touched her and called her 'sweetheart'.

What did it all mean?

Did he want to date her?

She liked him, aside from the whole captivity thing.

Hopefully, they would talk tonight when he returned, and he would tell her what was really going on.

The fluttery feeling in her belly returned as she sashayed into the kitchen. She turned on the radio, playing the upbeat 'I Wanna Dance with Somebody' by Whitney Houston.

Dancing and singing, she made an omelette. Ms Houston had been one of her mother's favourite artists.

She sat on a tall stool and ate breakfast at the counter. The music changed to more old school classics which she was beginning to enjoy because of Osagie.

She dropped her fork on the white porcelain plate, shocked by the realisation.

She knew Osagie musical and fashion taste well. She knew he owned nightclubs and bars.

Yet those were not solid foundations to build a relationship with a man who obviously lived a not-so-clean life.

What was he hiding from her?

A man his age would be married, right? He could have a wife—actually, scratch that. He could have several wives and children scattered around different locations. He'd practically boasted to her that he had a queue of women waiting to spend the night with him.

What if kidnapping women and making them fall in love with him was his kink? There were all kinds of narcissistic psychopaths out there. He could be one of them.

Why was she sitting here behaving as if her boyfriend had gone on a business trip, instead of trying to find out more about him and how she would escape?

She climbed down the stool.

It was just her in the house until Nathaniel returned or Idehen arrived at lunchtime. So, she could search the place for any clues. Perhaps she would find something to use as leverage against Osagie.

Ignoring the half-eaten omelette and coffee, she went searching, starting in the living room, opening drawers and cabinets. He had invaded her home and taken her. Invading his privacy was for her survival. She wouldn't be doing it if he hadn't taken her.

Still, she didn't have to go far. She found keys in a drawer and opened the door to one of the rooms she hadn't been in on the ground floor. The room was dark, the curtains drawn. She found the light switch on the wall and turned it on.

A gasp escaped her lips.

There were framed photographs stacked everywhere, different sizes. On the wall. On the floor. Osagie with a woman in a white gown. His wedding day? His wife? Osagie and the woman with a young child—a boy—in matching outfits.

The boy alone at different ages, from toddler to teenager.

Gina slumped into an armchair, clutching her chest.

Osagie had a family, a beautiful family.

And he'd hidden their photographs from Gina.

The lying, cheating sonofabitch.

He'd been so convincing this morning, kissing her, calling her 'sweetheart', looking at her as if she was the only woman on earth.

She'd nearly fallen for it too, foolish woman. She swiped angry tears from her face and stomped out of the room, slamming the door. She didn't want to look at all those happy faces.

Did his wife know that Osagie was a cheating asshole?

Did he really think Gina would never find out?

She was tempted to burn his fucking house down.

"Aarrgghhh," she growled.

If he thought she would sit here and play the good little woman, he had another think coming. She patted the card in her pocket. It would be her ticket to escaping Osagie.

She stomped up the stairs and went straight into the shower. She spent a long time in there, working out her plan.

Then she dressed in comfortable clothes, jeans, T-shirt, and sneakers. She would need to be able to move fast, even run, if necessary.

***

She was pacing the living room when Idehen arrived just after one o'clock. He didn't come into the house, and she followed him straight into the SUV. She hadn't seen him since that first day he'd brought food for her. She'd assumed he was a butler at the time. But the way he carried himself was less employee and more associate or friend?

He held the front passenger door. She climbed in and settled into the luxurious leather seats. Was this his car or Osagie's?

"Have you got everything you need?" he asked before starting the engine.

"Yes." She shifted to pat her bum where Osagie's card nestled in her pocket. She hadn't found where Osagie hid her phone or laptop. There was no point taking one of the purses he'd bought.

"And are you happy with the local mall or do you have a different one in mind."

"Can we go to Mega Mall? There will be better options for fashion outlets."

"Of course." He drove the car out of the house onto a quiet residential street with other houses surrounded by high fencing.

She would bet the people who lived in those houses were respectable. Yet one of their neighbours was a womanising kidnapper. She grunted in annoyance.

"Are you okay?" Idehen asked, glancing in her direction.

Shit. She'd forgotten she was in the car with one of her kidnappers.

"Oh, I'm fine. Just excited about going shopping." She tried to cover up her mistake, looking for a diversion. "How do you know Osagie?"

Idehen's mouth curved in a smile. "Osagie is family. We come from the same hometown and have known each other since we were boys."

"So, are you his friend or his employee?"

Idehen wasn't subservient even in front of Osagie. They seemed like equals. Yet he was running errands for the other man.

The man just shrugged. His gaze remained through the windscreen on the road ahead.

"What's the deal with Osagie abducting me. I mean a man like him can have anyone he wants. Why me?"

He glanced over, looking a little uncomfortable. "Yes, he can have anyone. You're special."

She laughed at the implication of his words.

"Special? Is he in love with me?" she asked jokingly.

A man like Osagie didn't know love. A man who took whatever he wanted. Who had no qualms about breaking into her apartment, drugging her, and taking her forcefully. He might be obsessed with her—a sinister obsession—but it wasn't loving.

Idehen stared at her with an expression she couldn't decipher. "You think being with him is bad? Trust me. There are worse things than being with Osagie."

Sure, there were people in worse situations, but this wasn't the life she wanted. She hadn't pictured she'd become someone's prized pet. No matter how stunning or generous they were. She had ambitions, a successful career in sports therapy, financial independence, perhaps even her own TV show one day.

When they arrived at the shopping mall, she sought the perfect opportunity to escape Idehen.

She chose the most expensive designer shop, which didn't have many customers.

"Osagie said I can have whatever I want, right?" she asked Idehen as she picked five cocktail dresses from different racks.

"Yes. Whatever you want," Idehen replied.

She nodded and asked the shop assistant for a changing room.

Idehen followed but didn't go through the door, since it was female only.

"Excuse me," Gina whispered to the personal shopper. "I need your help."

The woman entered the cubicle. "How can I help you?"

"That man you saw with me, kidnapped me and I need to escape. Can you help?" Gina kept glancing towards the door.

"What?" The woman's eyes bugged out.

"These people are well connected, and I really don't trust the police. I just need to get away. Please help me."

The girl backed away. "I'm not sure."

"It's simple. I just need to go out of the back door. Here—" She shoved the dresses in her arms at the shop assistant "—take these dresses to him and say that I selected them. Here are the card and the pin to pay for them and you will get the commission. The commission on the five dresses should be nice compensation on a quiet day. While he's distracted with paying, I can escape through the back door."

"You want to pay for all of these. Some are over $1000 each."

"Yes. The man out there is Idehen. Tell him that I'm just freshening up in the ladies and will be out shortly."

"Okay." The girl said with a shrug as she took the clothes.

"Where is the back door?" Gina asked, glancing towards the shop floor. She couldn't see Idehen from this angle.

"It's through there. It's a good thing my manager is at lunch. You can go now before anyone notices."

"Thank you." Gina slipped into the corridor and hurried towards the door with an exit sign at the top.

Heart thumping violently, she didn't look back, and she didn't stop. She pushed through into a stairwell, her sneakered feet pounding against the concrete, the sound echoing.

Panting, she ended up in the goods delivery bay. Stopped for a moment to catch her breath and get her bearings. Then she skirted the car park and onto the road.

She didn't have any money for public transport. She could hail a taxi to take her home and pay the driver when she got there. Best to avoid it, though, considering it would be the first place Idehen and his men would look for her.

She needed to go somewhere no one would think to look for her. Somewhere to lay low until she could figure out what to do.

Also, she needed to warn Dani, who was arriving tonight, not to go home. She could stay with Bolaji or someone else until the coast was clear.

Osagie had her phone. He had access to her contact list, so the stored addresses were ruled out, which meant no friends or family or colleagues.

Not trusting the police, she couldn't go there. Osagie probably had connections with law enforcement. Accusations wouldn't stick. She had no proof of his abduction. Not really. She wasn't injured or distressed. What would she say? That he abducted her, fed her, and gave her money to go shopping?

She didn't have cash or card for a hotel.

What was left?

Nigel.

Hell, no. Not him.

Who else?

Nigel lived within walking distance. No one would think she was there since she'd deleted his address from her contact list.

Still, he was the last person she wanted to see.

No. Right now, Osagie and any member of his team were the last people she wanted to see. Her ex-husband, Nigel, came second.

Nigel Banda had been her athletic coach for fourteen years and her husband for five of those years. Her father's friend had brought him along to her school sports day when she'd been seventeen years old. Nigel had seen her run. Afterwards, he'd told her she was brilliant could make it into the national team.

Two years later she'd been part of the team to participate in the African Athletics Championship in the 200m and 400m disciplines. She hadn't won any medals but had finished in fifth place in the

200m, fourth place and a personal record in the 400m, marking the start of her athletics career.

She'd been young and ambitious, training hard. Within five years, she'd become the African Champion and Commonwealth Champion. Then she'd married Nigel, and things started going wrong.

Nigel had been a great athletic coach but a crappy husband. They should never have married.

Gina sighed as the memories played back. She really didn't need her ex in her head.

Still, she had little choice.

He would help her. He owed her.

From his house, she would contact Dani and plan for a hotel until the danger passed.

Osagie's obsession would fade eventually. Hopefully.

This morning's kiss replayed in her mind. She'd nearly fallen for him, his charm, his smile, the gentle way he'd held her, kissed her.

For one moment this morning, she'd cast him as a hero.

But Osagie was no hero. He wasn't a knight who would sweep her off her feet and take away the pain of her mother's loss. He was a criminal. A man who made a living from illegal activities. To cap it all, he was married.

No matter how much he'd made her feel, how much he'd made her yearn, she needed to keep away from him.

It took over an hour to walk to the place. She stayed away from the main roads, using side streets, in case Idehen was looking for her. If she stayed vigilant, they wouldn't find her.

The Harmattan wind whipped sand and dust at her. Thankfully, she had warm clothes and comfortable sneakers.

When she turned into the familiar street, she exhaled a sigh. Glad, she hadn't been intercepted. She wasn't safe yet until she was inside the house.

The sky was orangish purple, the sun disappearing in the horizon when she arrived at her old residence.

Last she'd heard, Nigel still lived here, the home they'd shared. After she left him, she'd moved back to her parent's house.

She entered the building and ran up the stairs before pounding on the door of the first-floor apartment.

Nigel opened the door, wearing shorts and a tank top. "Gina?"

Middle-aged, he was balding and grey, his face showing wrinkles.

"Yes, it's me. Can I come in?" She darted her gaze down the stairs, making sure no one had seen her.

"Ehm. Sure." He stepped aside, and she hurried inside and entered the living room.

Not much had changed since her departure. The mint upholstered sofas, silver carpet and curtains. She'd decorated the place, but they now looked worn. The AC whirred, and the TV screen flickered on a sports channel.

Her chest squeezed tight. She'd once called this home.

Now another woman's photo hung on the wall.

She really shouldn't have come here. "Can I use your phone, please? I lost mine, and I need to contact my sister."

Nigel frowned and looked her over. "Oh. Are you okay? Sit down, please."

She lowered her body onto a sofa and closed her eyes in relief. "I'm okay. I'm sorry to intrude, but I won't stay long."

"It's not a problem. My phone's battery is dead, and I plugged it to recharge. We've had a power cut for days. So, I'm taking advantage of the electricity."

"Oh." Gina's heart jerked in her chest.

"Just give it a few minutes. What happened? Did you get robbed?"

"I lost my phone and my purse." She didn't want to tell him the truth because she didn't trust him that much. "Can I have some water, please? I've been walking for a while."

"That's terrible. Let me get you the drink." He left the room and came back with a bottle of water and a glass.

She drank two glasses before coming up for air. "How are Mary and your daughter?"

He'd married another of his prodigies. Except this one hadn't been as successful as Gina.

He averted his gaze, picking the remote controller. "Mary retrained as a nurse and moved to Canada."

Something didn't feel quite right. "So why aren't you spending Christmas with them?"

"I'm not a fan of the cold weather." He shrugged. "I just finished cooking when you came. Would you like to join me for dinner?"

Her stomach rumbled. She was hungry and tired. "I don't want to hassle you."

A loud crashing sound interrupted her, and she jumped upright.

"What the hell?"

"What was that?"

Two men stomped into the living room.

Shit.

Osagie.

Dressed in the navy suit and white shirt from this morning and holding a gun. He looked menacing and unforgiving, a dark angel on a mission.

What was he doing here? He'd been away on business. How had he gotten back so quickly?

Her mouth dried out, and she froze. Her heart nearly exploded through her chest.

"Go downstairs and get in the car, Georgina." The grim tone of Osagie's voice didn't inspire any challenge.

Breath bursting out of her, she felt rooted to the spot as her shoulders tightened.

How had he found Nigel's house? What would he do to her if she went downstairs? He'd promised not to hurt her. That was before she ran away.

"What are you doing in my house? Get out!" Nigel said in an annoyed voice.

Pfft. Osagie fired his weapon.

Gina flinched, body trembling, leg muscles tightening. She was ready to run again.

Nigel cried out and crumpled to the ground.

"No!" She flopped beside him, checking him over.

There was a bullet hole in his leg.

"He didn't do anything. Why did you shoot him?" she cried, ready to throw up whatever was left in her empty stomach.

"I told you no one needed to get hurt as long as you do what I say. If you don't want me to put a bullet through his head, get in the car. Now." Osagie pointed the glinting weapon at Nigel who clutched his thigh where blood seeped through his fingers.

"Fine. I'll go with you but let me make sure he doesn't bleed to death." She hurried into the kitchen and came back with a towel which she wrapped around the wound.

"I'm sorry," she muttered to the Nigel. "Call one of the neighbours to take you to the hospital."

The neighbours were probably on the way to find out what all the commotion was about.

She shouldn't have come here. She'd brought trouble to Nigel's doorstep.

Walking stiffly, she followed another of Osagie's security team down the stairs.

Idehen stood by the car, holding the back door open, shaking his head at her.

Feeling numb and tired, Gina climbed into the back seat. She'd been running away from Osagie for hours. No food. Little water. Just when freedom seemed within reach, he'd recaptured her.

He'd already shot Nigel. What would he do to her?

Minutes later, Osagie got into the back seat beside her. He didn't say anything as the chauffeur drove down the dusty street back onto the highway.

Hands jammed into her armpits, she sat huddled in the corner. For the first time since she met him, she feared for her life.

SIX

THERE WERE WORSE things than death.

Gina sat like a statue in the back seat of the luxury SUV for the longest drive of her life. A shaking sculpture with beads of sweat trickling down her face, dampening her top while her hands were jammed under clammy armpits. Her sneakered foot bounced on the floor mat.

Although she occasionally managed to take a long drag to quell her body's tremors for a few seconds, breath burst in and out of her.

Osagie sat on the other side of the middle armrest he'd lowered, ensuring there was no accidental contact between them.

Not speaking to her, he conversed in Edo language with Idehen who sat in the front passenger seat beside Nekpen, the chauffeur.

Osagie's intoxicating cologne and musk scented the air, reminding her of this morning—his sensual kiss, his stimulating embrace, his delightful promise.

How did a day that started on a wonderful note go so wrong? What offences did she commit, warranting this current situation?

Less than a week ago, her pressing concerns had been dealing with a plumbing problem at the gym.

Now her primary interest was surviving Christmas Eve at the hands of gangsters.

What a rollercoaster week it had been.

The attraction of meeting Osagie in the park. The fear of waking up to him in her room. The adrenaline of fighting and running. The panic of encountering his dogs. The comfort of his arms in the aftermath. The laughter of sharing meals and his company. The anticipation after this morning's kiss and the terror of watching him shoot a man.

If she'd been confused about what kind of man Osagie was, seeing him shoot Nigel without hesitation or flinching confirmed precisely what he was—ruthless, brutal, and forceful.

A man who wasn't afraid of the law, who took the law into his hands.

Although she hoped not, Nigel could inform the police about his injury and press charges.

How would she explain what happened if she survived the night?

About an hour after leaving Nigel's flat, Nekpen drove into premises Gina didn't recognise, through a raised barrier to a secluded underground parking spot.

Osagie left the car without talking to Gina. Nekpen didn't get out.

Idehen came around and opened the door for her.

Heart rate skyrocketing, Gina stepped out and took a deep breath.

"Where are we?" she asked in a croaky whispery voice.

She'd thought they would go back to Osagie's house. He'd been calm and even affectionate there. She'd been hoping he would be more forgiving there too.

Instead, this place lit by flickering white, fluorescent bulbs had dark, creepy corners. She couldn't imagine Osagie being gentle or compassionate here.

She'd watched enough movies where people were shot in spaces like this. Shivering, she braced her arms around her body. How was she going to get out of this mess?

"This way." Idehen pointed in the direction of a white door at the far corner.

Osagie walked about five paces ahead. His footsteps clipped and echoed, his expression stony and silent. He appeared disappointed, hurt.

She followed him, regret made her feel uneasy. Shoulders sagging, her gut twisted as she walked beside Idehen.

Swallowing the big lump in her throat, she focused blankly on the grey walls as they climbed the concrete stairs to the first floor.

Idehen held the door for her to enter a wide corridor. Footsteps echoed off the concrete surface. On either side were rooms with glass walls and doors.

In one, a naked woman was on her knees while a man face-fucked her.

Gina's cheeks heated, and she turned in the other direction only to watch two women with strap-ons spit-roasting a man over a bench.

Her body flushed. What the hell was this place? She hurried along and all through the hallway, each room had some sexual activity going on.

Osagie rounded the corner into an open space with benches that looked like a waiting area.

Gina followed and halted, heart racing. A sudden coldness hit her core.

A man and woman knelt on the concrete floor, cuffed, and chained by the far wall.

Gina couldn't see their faces because Osagie obscured her view. She ambled to the side to see better, her stomach rolling.

"Dani?" Gina exclaimed in shock.

Her sister's gaze flicked up, met Gina's and her skin paled.

"Oh, God," Dani whimpered, breaking eye contact and hugging her midriff. She looked unkempt, hair dishevelled, clothes askew and sweat dripping from her forehead.

Bolaji knelt beside her, shifting uncomfortably, and looking everywhere but at Gina.

"What is going on here?" Gina asked, moving towards her sister.

"Madaki, here are the trio," Osagie said, ignoring her question. "How much do you think you can get for them at the auction."

A slender, dark-skinned man in mauve tunic and trousers suit who'd been sitting on a metal chair near a grey metal table stood. "I need them all to strip so I can examine the merchandise."

Gina's brows shot upwards. Strip? Who was stripping? "Osagie, what's going on?"

He swivelled and shoved hands into his pockets. "Your sister and her boyfriend stole from me and disappeared. I took you because I needed to track them down. Now, she claims she doesn't have my money, and he claims he spent it. They owe me twenty thousand dollars."

"Twenty Grand? What, the Hell?" Gina's head whipped around in her sister's direction. "Dani? Is this true? Did you steal from Mr Peters?"

Dani avoided her gaze. "I don't know what I was thinking. Bolaji told—"

"It's not true," Bolaji cut in, shaking his head. "I didn't tell you anything."

"Stop lying. It was your idea—"

A shot ricocheted, making everyone freeze.

"I don't give a fuck whose idea it was. You dared to steal from me, and you're going to pay for it. Madaki, do your assessment." Osagie swivelled and walked towards the door.

A man grabbed Gina's arm, dragging her towards the back of the room. She panicked, her stomach lurched. Was Osagie going to leave her here?

"Osagie, wait," she shouted.

He kept walking.

"Please!"

He stopped and turned, his expression cold. "What?"

She swallowed the bile in her throat. "What's going on? Why am I here?"

"You're here because you owe me Eight Grand."

"Eight Grand? How do I owe you money?" she screeched in shock.

"You spent my four thousand dollars on dresses you had no intentions of wearing. Do I look like a money-miss-road to you? I want my fucking money back, with interest. Between the three of you, you owe me almost Thirty Gees and Mr Madaki will sell you at auction to his clients so I can get some of my money back."

"Auction? Oh, Lord." She grabbed her head. What had she done? "You're really serious. You're going to sell us like cattle. What kind of monster are you?"

He expression was an implacable mask. "I never claimed to be a good person. Unlike you and your sister who pretend to be good and yet you are thieves and liars."

Her cheeks heated. He was right. He had shown how dangerous he was when he invaded her home. She had made up fantasies about him being good.

But he had been compassionate. His response after his dogs scared Gina, showed he must have a heart. Maybe she could appeal to that side of him again. What other option was there? She had to get out of here with her sister intact. Her sister was her blood, her last surviving close family. She couldn't let anything happen to Dani.

She had to make Osagie stay and listen. If he left, they would never get out of here.

She walked up to him and knelt in front of him. "I'm sorry."

Sighing heavily, Osagie's palm settled at the back of her neck. He gripped her head, tilting it back, so she looked up at his hardened face. "I don't trust you."

"Give me a chance to rebuild your trust. Please don't sell my sister or me."

He laughed derisively. "Do you really think you have that much control over me? That if you just flutter your lashes, pout your lips, beg me, I'll let you go? Do you fucking know what I am? What I do for a living? You're just pussy. One pussy is as good as the next."

She sucked in a harsh breath, lungs constricting.

Okay. He was mean. She'd hurt him by running, and he was hurting her in return with his words. She could see it in his eyes.

Best to just shake it off. There was no room for pride here—only survival.

"I might be just pussy. And you might have had tons of them. But you haven't had this one. If you put me up for auction, you'll never get to taste me. And I know you want me."

He gripped her neck, yanked her upright and crushed her back to the wall. She struggled to inhale.

His hot breath whispered against her ear. "I thought you were intelligent, Georgina. Taunting me in front of my men? Do you really want to play for an audience? Because I can fuck you right here in front of everyone and still put you up for auction. Want to dare me?"

Her pulse skyrocketed, and she felt breathless.

Shit. A man who owned a sex club wouldn't have a problem with public displays. Okay. Maybe she shouldn't have taunted him with sex. Perhaps he hadn't sold her already because he hadn't had sex with her.

"I'm sorry. Please, don't leave me here. I'll do whatever you want me to do." She wasn't afraid of him. But she feared what would happen if he left.

A bitter smile curled his lips, and his dark brow rose. "You will?"

"Yes."

"Prove it."

She stared at him, knowing she'd do whatever he asked just to get out of this place. Away from the men watching her, giving her the creeps.

He put his hand inside his jacket, pulled out his handgun and placed it into her palm. She nearly dropped it from shock and the weight.

Osagie still held onto the gun in her hand and pointed in Bolaji's direction. "Shoot that bastard."

"What? No!" Gina had briefly dated an Olympic Shooting Sports athlete. The man had taken her to his home and shown his gun collection. He'd even taught her how to fire a weapon. However, she'd never been comfortable with his obsession with guns, so she'd stopped seeing him.

"You've got to be shitting me," Bolaji said in a shaking jokey voice. His eyes darted around the space and landed on Gina, his mouth in a half-smile half-grimace.

Dani's eyes bulged in disbelief.

Osagie tilted her head and held her gaze with an intense look. No amusement tinged his expression. "Prove that I can trust you. Show me where your loyalties lie. Me or him."

Fuck! The whoosh of rushing blood sounded so loud in Gina's ears, and her vision blurred a little.

Osagie turned the gun in her hand toward his chest.

Licking her lips, Gina stared from Osagie to Bolaji.

She must have been delirious or something. It had to be because she was tired, her body sore, and needed a drink of water. She wasn't reasoning.

She had a gun in her hand pointed at the man who had abducted her. She could release the safety, pull the trigger, and kill him.

Still, she couldn't do it. Couldn't hurt him. She cared for him.

He'd taken care of her, in his dark, peculiar way. In Osagie's own way.

Somehow she could trust Osagie to protect her. He'd done so already.

Bolaji was doing the opposite to her sister. He'd gotten Dani into trouble. And wasn't even man enough to own up to his mistakes.

Gina twisted the gun in Bolaji's general direction.

He scrambled on the floor. "Gina, no!"

"You listen to me, Bolaji. You are going to pay Mr Peters every dollar you stole from him."

"What? No way."

All the stress of the past week crashed in on her. She'd had enough of all this nonsense.

She clicked the safety and pulled the trigger.

Crack!

The bullet blasted into the wall behind Bolaji.

"Gina!" Dani crouched into a ball.

Bolaji scrambled back, and a dark patch appeared on his trouser crotch area. Did he just pee himself?

Gina twisted her face in disgust, adrenaline rushing through her.

"Listen up, you little shit of a man." Gina stepped up and crouched in front of Bolaji and Dani, gun still levelled at Bolaji's head. "I've had enough of your bullshit. And the same goes to you, Dani. This ends now. The two of you will pay back every freaking dollar you stole, do you hear me?"

"Yes. Okay. Yes," Dani said, covering her face with her hand.

"Look at me," Gina ordered.

Her sister sniffled and lowered her hand from her face. She stared at Gina as if seeing her for the first time.

Gina supposed she saw a different person, not the calm, docile person she was used to overrunning. Somehow, having a gun in her hand made Gina feel powerful in a way she'd never felt before. She could understand why men like Osagie carried them.

"You are going to sell off every designer bag and shoe and wig and anything else of value you have to pay back that money."

"Gina, it's me o. Your sister," Dani sniffled, trying to play the innocent.

Gina pushed off the floor, angrily. "What do you think mum and dad would have done to you if they were here?"

"I'm sorr—"

"I'm serious, Dani. You're going to pay that money back. Our parents didn't raise thieves."

"Yes. Yes. I'll pay back the money." Dani looked crestfallen.

Gina turned to Bolaji. "Same goes for you. You will give back every cent. If you can't do that, then Mr Peters has my permission to do whatever he likes with you."

"You can't make me!" he said, glaring at her.

"Oh, you watch me and see. And you will keep away from my sister, or I swear to God I will shoot you myself. Now crawl over to Mr Peters and apologise. Promise you'll never do it again."

"What?"

"Fucking, do it!" She released another bullet into the far wall.

Both her sister and Bolaji sniffled and shuffled and crawled across the concrete floor to where Osagie stood, watching the proceedings with an inscrutable expression.

"I'm sorry," Bolaji mumbled.

"Sorry or not. You owe me money, mister, and I'm giving you a month to pay it off. Next time you won't be walking away. Get out of here, now," Osagie commanded.

A man appeared from the shadows, released the chain, and escorted Bolaji out.

"I'm so sorry for stealing your money, Mr Peters. I promise I won't do it again," Dani said.

Osagie looked at Dani on the floor and then at Gina.

Gina met his gaze. "You can assign her to do whatever job you want her to do, unpaid, of course, until the value of the debt is paid. She will sign an agreement to that effect."

Osagie shook his head. "Her signature is worth shit."

"I'll co-sign it," Gina said.

Osagie's brows rose in surprise. "That means you'll become liable for her debt if she absconds."

"Well, I'm liable now anyway."

"Fair enough. We are agreed. I'll send you the document by email." His tilted his head. "I don't have to tell you that no law officials should be involved in this matter. You are free to go, both of you."

He stretched out his hand, and Gina handed the gun over.

"Thank you," she said, exhaling in relief. This could have gone a lot worse.

"Idehen, make sure they get home safely," Osagie said and headed towards the door. "See you around, Georgina."

He disappeared without looking back.

Georgina stood frozen, disorientated, and deflated as the adrenaline in her system crashed. Dani scrambled off the floor.

He was gone, just like that. No goodbye. Nothing.

What was all that this morning about missing her? Okay. She'd run away. But she'd apologised, hadn't she?

"Where is Osagie going?" Gina asked Idehen.

"To his office."

"He works here?"

"He owns the buildings in this block."

"Oh. So, the nightclub is here?"

"Yes. Next door."

"Okay. Show me how to get to the club and take my sister home."

"What?" Dani said. "You can't go to the club. Mr Peters said we should go home."

When she had a quiet moment, she would analyse what drove her to wave a gun at her sister and Bolaji. Why she lost her temper? But for now, Gina had unanswered questions, and she wasn't going home until she got them.

"I know what he said. But I have something to do. Idehen, show me. And by the way, do you still have the card from the shopping trip?"

She had no money for the entry fee. Since she already owed Osagie, a little more wouldn't hurt.

"Yes." Idehen frowned.

"Okay. Let me have it."

"I need to return it to Osagie." He dipped a hand into his pocket and pulled out a brown leather wallet.

"Well, I will personally give it to him," she said, extending her arm.

He placed the card into her palm and then led the way back to the foyer where they walked through a hallway connecting two buildings.

They entered another foyer with a black-uniformed bouncer and shiny dark surfaces. Thumping music vibrated through the soles of the sneakers.

"Madam, you can't come in dressed like that," the bouncer said.

She wasn't exactly dressed for clubbing, in the dusty jeans and T-shirt she'd been in all day.

"Let her in. She is Mr Peters' guest," Idehen said from behind her.

"Okay, sir," the bouncer replied and held the door.

"Gina, are you sure about this?" Dani held her arm as if to stop her from entering the venue. "Arufin is not your kind of nightclub."

"I'm sure," Gina said curtly, shrugging her hand off." I'll see you later."

What did her sister know about her kind of nightclub anyway? She'd proven tonight that she could get out of her comfort zone.

She entered the club without looking back. Cold air blasted onto her skin as soon as she stepped in.

The place was jam-packed with people in every corner, most of them were skimpily clothed. The bar counter took up the whole of the far wall with about eight bartenders serving customers. A DJ played afrobeat from his deck on a mezzanine level to the right. A dancefloor with gyrating revellers stood directly below. Almost naked men and women danced in cages hung from the high ceiling. Strobe lighting flashed repeatedly. While in the far-left corner where secluded areas created by low and intimate lighting.

She walked towards the crowded bar and waited her turn to reach the counter. Glancing back, she noticed another mezzanine hanging over the entrance, which seemed to be a VIP area. Another bouncer stood by the cordoned-off section.

Eventually, a bartender faced her. "What would you like, madam?"

"Vodka and Coke," she replied, shouting to be heard above the thumping music.

"Coming up." He reached for a glass and mixed her request.

She tapped the card to pay.

He checked the receipt, then Gina, and spoke to a colleague before turning away to fiddle with his phone.

Gina pretended she didn't see what he was doing and picked the drink. She took a deep gulp before turning to face the crowd again.

She'd set the ball rolling. It was only a matter of time before Osagie took the bait. Hopefully.

SEVEN

OSAGIE'S FOOTSTEPS were muted by the thumping music's baseline as he made his way to his personal lounge on the second floor of Club Arufin.

He had a fully functional office in the adjacent building. However, he preferred to conduct business in the informal atmosphere of the lounge.

"Good evening, Mr Peters." His assistant dressed in a navy business skirt-suit approached. "Madam Sophie is waiting in the lounge for you."

"Okay. Thank you." He pushed the door and held it so his assistant could enter.

"Hello, Sophie." He stretched his hands out for a shake.

The woman was dressed in a tight-fitting black outfit that showed off her bountiful assets front and back, set off by the stilettos. Her long extensions pulled back in a low ponytail. She dressed for maximum effect.

Osagie didn't miss the confident way she came across and shook his hand.

"Hi, Mr Peters. Thank you for taking the time to see me. I understood you would not be here for this meeting."

"It's not a problem. My business trip got cut short, so I had some available time. Please sit." He waved at the leather settees.

Sophie settled into the one she'd vacated. "We were wrapping up the meeting. Your assistant, Remi, has already explained your requirements for the Grand Prix weekends. And I've explained that our service can supply clean, high-end escorts for the events. I've also explained that as per our contract, the escorts are not to be marked and any extra activities beyond companionship have to be consensual."

"That's fair enough."

"Thanks again for your time, Mr Peters." Sophie stood.

"You're welcome. I look forward to doing more business with the Odili family. By the way, I presume you will be at the New Year's Eve party."

"Of course I'll be there."

"See you there. Have a good evening."

"You, too."

His assistant ushered Sophie out while Osagie checked his buzzing phone. He opened the message from Idehen.

Gina is in Arufin.

What?

Standing, he dialled the number to call his friend, while he scanned the floor below.

Even though it was Christmas Eve, the place was packed the same as it was almost every night. It was the most popular bar in Lori Osa. He had other business interests, but this was his golden cash cow.

The ultra-modern atmosphere attracted attention. Bodies writhed on the dance floor, every person having to pay a door fee. Not to talk about the amount of alcohol and other intoxicants that flowed and lined his profits. Celebrities vied to acquire the exclusive VIP cards, while musicians wanted the chance to play here.

Osagie had been in the nightclub business for many years before he'd discovered the ground-breaking formula that became Arufin, the most successful of all his clubs.

"You're on speakerphone. I'm driving," Idehen said as soon as he answered the call.

"Why is Gina at Arufin? I told you to take her home," Osagie forewent the preamble as well.

"She refused. She insisted on going into the club after you left. I gave her your card. I'm taking her sister home."

Osagie growled, his gaze scanning the dance floor and bar areas that were visible.

A woman in a dark T-shirt turned away from the bar carrying a drink in her hand.

Georgina.

"I see her," he said into the phone.

"And?" Idehen asked as if expecting a running commentary.

"And a muthafucker just approached her. He's standing too fucking close to her."

"It's a nightclub. People stand close to each other." There was amusement in Idehen's voice.

"I know that, dammit." He scrubbed a hand over his scalp and lifted his gaze to the ceiling that had little LEDs embedded into it, creating a starry effect.

He glanced back into the bar below. "Now she's laughing at whatever the fool said in her ear. I'm going to kill him."

The sound of a giggly voice on the phone took him unawares. "Who the fuck is that?"

"I told you I was taking Daniella home."

"Oh." So engrossed in Georgina, he'd forgotten Dani could hear the conversation.

"Anyway, don't go committing murder tonight. It'll be too messy to clean and too many witnesses to shut up," Idehen said in a teasing manner.

"Whatever, man. I'll talk to you later." He ended the call only to see another message from Rayo, the bar manager downstairs.

Boss, there's a lady down here using your card. Should I put her drinks on your tab?

He sent a reply. *No. Bring her to my lounge.*

Yes, Sir. The reply came almost immediately.

Osagie stood there and watched as the bar manager approached the chatting couple. He said something after which Gina glanced up at the second level. While he could see the rest of the floors, they couldn't see him through the glass in addition to the heavy shadows.

Anticipation danced in her eyes as if she expected to see him. Then, she dropped her head and followed Rayo.

Osagie remained standing, impatience coiling in his stomach.

What was Georgina playing at? Was she trying to goad him, into what?

First, she had run away. When Idehen had called to say she had bribed a store assistant to use their back entrance to escape, Osagie's gut had wrenched.

A day ago, he might have understood, might have accepted her need to escape so readily. After all, he'd taken her for the purposes of drawing her sister out.

However, after this morning and the kiss they'd shared, after he'd told her how much he cared for her, he'd thought they could move beyond what had brought them together in the first place. He'd even considered writing off Daniella's debt as a Christmas gift to Georgina.

He would have done it too when she'd said she was looking forward to his return home. Meanwhile, she'd been planning to run away.

His hands balled into fists. Good thing he'd allowed Georgina to go shopping and she'd shown her true intentions. Sending her with Idehen had been a test. He'd had a backup all along. Her sneakers had a GPS tracker, designed for an athlete to keep track of steps and distances covered. But it also worked as a monitoring device and showed real-time locations on a digital map.

And worse, she'd gone to *him*—that shithead of an ex-husband-slash-sports-coach of hers.

Hence, his fury.

He could accept Georgina running away. In her shoes, he might have done the same thing.

But out of all the people she could've gone to for safety, she had chosen Mr Banda.

As soon as Osagie discovered where she was headed, he had to walk away from her. He couldn't let history repeat itself.

No, he wasn't going back there. One woman tearing his heart out in this lifetime was enough.

Now, Gina was in his club.

She didn't fit into his world, which was the reason he hadn't touched her although he'd wanted to from that first day he'd seen her.

She'd been a breath of fresh air in his home over the past week, a place he hadn't entertained female company since his wife left.

She'd made him feel things, made him crave things he hadn't thought he'd need again.

Her intelligence. Her sass. Her openness. Her body.

He was attracted to everything she had to offer.

And tonight, just seeing the way she had handled the weapon and nearly pistol-whipped Bolaji into compliance. Damn. So, fucking sexy. He'd been hard in an instant.

As much as he wanted her, there was nothing Osagie Peters couldn't walk away from.

That was the key to survival.

Don't get attached to anything. Never again.

So, he had to stop whatever game Gina was playing.

Granted, a woman hadn't captured his attention for a while, not since Xandra.

His sexual encounters with the assassin had been enjoyable. However, she was now involved in a stable and happy relationship with a rancher up in Bakili. Osagie had wished her well. She deserved love and happiness after everything that she'd been through.

Ah, he sighed. He was getting sappy in his old age.

The ding of a bell indicated someone was at the door before it pushed in, and Gina appeared at the threshold.

"Rayo, thank you," Osagie said.

Georgina corked her hip, crossed an arm under her chest while holding the other from which she sipped a dark liquid in a clear plastic tumbler. She didn't acknowledge him.

The open door let in the sound of thumping music.

A swift jab of annoyance made Osagie grimace.

Gina looked at him and broke into giggles, the sound replacing the music once the door shut with Rayo's departure.

"You should see your face," she said, still laughing. "If you hate this music so much, why do you own a nightclub?"

"Because young people like this sterile, digital auto-tuned crap where you can't identify the artist by their voice or style. It's so homogenous. Give me the psychedelic Fela or soulful Anita or the range of Mariah or raspy Macy any day."

"God, you're so old." She snickered.

Warmth bloomed in his chest, and he nearly cracked a smile.

Then the image of her cradling her ex-husband made his gut harden into stone. His anger returned.

"What the fuck are you doing in my club?" his voice was gruff.

She shrugged. "It's a free country. I can go wherever I like."

"The Hell you can. Not in my club."

"What? Am I barred from Arufin?" The bullet tips of her nipples were outlined in her fitted shirt.

"You bet your ass, you are barred from all of my clubs."

Her eyes widened. She placed the cup on a sideboard close to the door and crossed her arms over her chest, blocking the taut nipples from view.

Just as well.

Osagie needed to get his mind off Georgina's body. But when she was this close, breathing the same air as him, it was near impossible.

"Why?"

Her question jarred him from his thoughts. "What?"

"Why am I barred from Arufin?"

"It's my club. I can bar whomever I please."

"Not good enough." She shook her head and walked towards him.

"Say that again." He must have misheard her. She didn't just tell him what he thought she said.

"I said your reason is not good enough. Try again." She held his gaze, challenging him to do his worst, arms akimbo.

Damn.

His mouth dropped open. It was his turn to be speechless.

Only two people had dared challenge him previously—Idehen and Xandra.

Idehen was a brother-in-arms, a partner-in-crime, the most trusted person he had in his inner circle. They'd known each long enough for the man to call bullshit on him.

Admittedly, he had a soft spot for Xandra. She'd been a reflection of him when he'd first met her—the distrustful nature, directness, pain, and yearning for something out of reach.

If he picked up the phone and called Xandra, she would show up for him. The same way Idehen would show up, without question.

Was it possible that he could add Georgina to the list?

No. She'd proven that she couldn't be trusted.

He wasn't going to give her another chance. He never gave second chances.

"Georgina, I'm done talking to you. I'll send one of the boys to take you home." He reached for his phone on the table.

"No. I'm not going anywhere. I'm not done talking to you," she said insolently.

He narrowed his eyes. "Are you sure you're okay? Because it seems you've forgotten to whom you're talking."

"I know exactly who I'm talking to—Osagie Peters, businessman, sex club owner, shooter of men, kidnapper of women."

Okay. That almost made him laugh.

But she didn't stop her rant. "Do you think that you can turn up to my house, snatch me in the middle of the night, keep me locked away for days, make me spend time with you, make me like you, only for you to suddenly just toss me aside like I'm a piece of dirty rag? If that is your intention, then you picked the wrong fucking woman."

"Georgina," her name was a growl on his lips as he stood. "I'm warning you. Don't test my patience. You kissed me this morning. Hours later, you ran away and returned to your ex-husband. So, I'm not buying this shit you're pulling. Go home."

Every time the image of her and Nigel replayed in his mind, his chest hurt as if he replayed his wife's betrayal.

"I ran because I saw pictures of your wife and son."

He narrowed his eyes, hands balling into fists. "How? Those photographs are locked away."

"I know. I found the key and unlocked the room." She averted her gaze, looking shamefaced for a few seconds. Then she glared at him. "Anyway, you broke into my home and took stuff without my permission. So, I guess we're even on that note. The point is, you have a wife, and you returned my kiss—"

"I don't have a fucking wife. She cheated on me. I kicked her out. Case closed."

"Oh. I'm sorry."

"Don't be. Just go."

She didn't move. She stood there, head tilted, watching him.

He ignored her, grabbed his phone, and dialled his chauffeur, Nekpen. The man answered in one ring. "Boss?"

"Ms Georgina Badu is coming down. You'll take her home," he said.

"Which of the homes, sir?"

"Her home. You remember where that is?"

"Yes, Boss."

"Good." Osagie hung up.

"The car is ready for you," he said to Gina.

"Let me get this straight. You kidnap me to use as bait to trap my sister, and I'm expected to forgive you. Yet you can't forgive me for running away and trying to save myself."

"No. First, I'm not asking you to forgive me for kidnapping you. I'd do it again if the situation reoccurred. Also, I enjoyed your company while it lasted. Secondly, I have no problem with you running away. If I had been in your shoes, I would have done the same thing."

She narrowed her eyes. "So, what is this about? Why are you sending me away?"

He turned his head so she couldn't see how much she'd hurt him. "Of all the places you could have gone for safety, you chose your ex, and then you cradle him like he's the most important person to you, right in front of me."

Georgina hadn't even tried to hide her feelings for the man. It had felt like walking in on his ex-wife and her lover.

"Oh," she said as if stunned by his words. "I only went to Nigel as a last resort. It was a bad idea. He means nothing to me except as ex-coach and ex-husband."

Something fluttered in Osagie's chest. Still, he tamped it down. She shouldn't be here. He met her gaze with a stony expression.

"It doesn't matter. Look around you. Have you forgotten? I'm a monster, a shooter of men and a kidnapper of women. If you think I'm going to change, you're wasting your time. I'm not good enough for you."

She shook her head, lips twisted.

"No. You don't get to tell me who is good enough for me. Sure, selling people is screwed up. Then again, if someone stole my money, I'd probably do something to them just as bad. My sister shouldn't have stolen from you. Period. Still, we're where we are."

She took a step towards him, eyes challenging him. "Mr Peters, you picked me. Now, I pick you. You're not getting rid of me that easily, even if it means I must apply through one of those stupid apps to get your attention. Not-so-little Red is in the evil forest to claim the wolf. What are you going to do about it?"

Fuck. Georgina was here to claim him. A first.

He groaned as his cock throbbed. The way she used his formal name and her determination made him as hard as a rock and chafing against his boxers' thin fabric.

As if she knew what she'd done, her eyes went wide and she swiped her bottom lips with a pink tongue.

He stifled another groan. This was new for him.

Women didn't have this effect on him. Not this unrestrained desire, this lustful itch that was at risk of driving him to breaking point.

The thing was, she was fully clothed in jeans, a T-shirt, and sneakers. Yet, the fabric moulded her body in perfection.

He saw naked bodies frequently in the club. None of them ever threatened to shatter his control in this manner.

He'd tried to avoid this. However, Georgina seemed determined to be claimed by him.

And once she became his...

Oh, there would be consequences—no escaping it.

Once she stepped into his world, his enemies would have a weakness against him. He would become a visible target, and so many would use her to bring him down.

And once she became his, he would fight, he would kill, to protect her.

The thought only made him more determined.

"No need, Georgina. Your wish has been granted. You sailed through the screening process, and now you get to experience what it means to belong to me. I should warn you, I don't share."

"Neither do I. If you cheat on me, I will cut off your balls." She didn't even flinch.

He believed every word, after what he'd seen her do to Bolaji and Dani. His Georgina was a badass goddess, and he was ready to worship at her altar.

"Good. We understand each other. Now for the devouring." He grinned wolfishly.

She understood his meaning. Her eyes bulged, and she glanced at the door, backing away.

A smirk twisted his lips as he stalked her. "The door is locked. There's nowhere to run."

"Oh, I disagree." Her gaze flitted across the room as if searching for an escape route. Yet, the twinkle in her eyes showed she wasn't afraid.

Yes. Georgina's playfulness only made his raging hard, aching erection nearly split the zipper of his trousers. He was ready to play. But first.

"What's your safe word?" he asked.

She halted, glanced at him curiously. "Safe word?"

"Yes. You know what that is, right?" He hoped he didn't have to start from scratch with her.

"Of course, I know what it is. I got curious about you and educated myself on sex clubs and kinks."

"Clever woman." He grinned. He could get on with what he wanted to do. "So, your safe word is?"

"Ehm. I don't have one. How about red to stop, yellow to take a break and green to go all the way?"

"Perfect because I'm about to fuck you, all the way." He straightened.

"Here?" The pulse on her collar jumped, and she licked her bottom lip again.

"Right here, sweetheart. Are you afraid?"

"No. I have an urge to run. But I want you to catch me."

"Then, run," he ordered.

She yelped and rushed in the other direction towards the fire exit.

He moved fast, hurdled over the sofa, and cut off her escape route.

She jerked to a halt, swivelled, changing direction, rushing across the private lounge towards his office door.

Heart thumping hard, he gave chase. He was fast and knew the corners and obstacles better than she did. As she reached the door, he caught her shoulder and yanked.

She crashed into his chest, squealing. Squirming, she pushed, using the wall as leverage to escape.

He wrapped an arm around her waist, holding her back to his front.

"You like to run. I like to chase," he whispered in a husky voice against her ear.

In response, she rolled her hips, rubbing her cushiony bum against his throbbing erection.

Tilting his head back, he groaned, his grip on her slackening.

"Don't celebrate. You haven't caught me yet," Georgina teased and slipped out.

He didn't let her get far. He caught her against the glass screen overlooking the club two floors below.

He crushed her front to his, her back against the thick Perspex. They were both panting, chests heaving.

He cupped her chin, tilting her head so he could look in her eyes. "I have you now."

Before she could reply, he crushed her lips with his.

And his world tipped upside down. There was no going back.

The kiss was a lighter to the fuel simmering in his veins. She tasted sweet, heavenly, more than he'd imagined.

He was lost, kissing her hungrily, devouring her mouth.

Georgina moaned, her body trembled, her arms reaching up and wrapping around his neck. She wriggled and arched, making the most beautiful sounds he'd ever heard.

His blood roared hot, and he deepened the kiss, twirling around. They bumped into the back of a sofa.

He grunted, breaking the kiss to look her over. "Are you okay?"

"Green, Mr Peters." She seemed to have gotten the hang of the traffic light code. The light danced in her teasing eyes as she slipped away.

He shot his hand out, grabbed, and tackled her. They crashed onto the carpet. In a swift wrestling move, she flipped and landed onto his chest, trying to pin him.

Damn, she was strong and beautiful and athletic.

And she was making him hard enough to pound concrete.

He reached up and took her left nipple into his mouth and sucked, wetting the T-shirt and bra in the process.

"Not fair." She let out a long moan, arching her body and pushing the breast further into his mouth.

He took advantage and overturned, her back to the carpet, his bulk pressing onto her.

"All's fair in love and war." He tugged her arms up, trapping her hands together with his.

She froze and stared at him with concentration. "Is that what this is? War?"

Was she asking if this was love, indirectly?

He didn't know. Just knew he wanted her here and now. And tomorrow. And the day after that. But he'd been burned before and wasn't going to give his heart away again.

He answered it in the same indirect manner. "Time will tell."

He tugged her T-shirt, and she lifted her upper body, letting him take it off and toss it over the sofa. Her fleshy breasts filled out the sheer black bra. Her toned abs could make any hardened gym rat jealous.

God, she was beautiful. He wanted to watch, touch, and taste her all at once. Again, and again.

He concentrated on taking her jeans off as she shimmied and wriggled to help him, kicking her sneakers off too.

It had been so long since he'd been this excited to be with a woman. He didn't want to overanalyse the reasons.

He tossed the clothes, turned to her, and nearly came in his trousers.

Only a flimsy scrap of black silk fabric covered her pussy. Her body was lush and toned cinnamon, her hips wide, her legs extended. She was tempting and gorgeous, and it seemed, all his, for tonight at least.

He groaned, squeezing his eyes shut to get some control back. "Sweetheart, you're driving me insane."

"So are you, Mr Peters." She reached for his buttons, fingers grazing his chest through the shirt.

He clamped her hands together. "No. Not yet."

He reached under the sofa and tugged the black leather cuffs attached to a metal bolt on the floor.

Gina gasped as she stared at the cuffs. Her body shook, and her breath came out in rasps.

Osagie couldn't tell if she was afraid or excited. This was a good time for a verbal cue since he'd introduced a new variable.

"What traffic light are we at, sweetheart?" He held still, willing his body to calm so he could remain in control.

She eyed the cuffs, then him. "Yellow, Mr Peters."

He returned the cuffs to the floor, sitting on his heels. "Have you ever been tied up during sex?"

"No." Her gaze trailed over his body. "I'm not afraid of being tied up. Yes, I want to wear your cuffs. But I want you to make me wear them. I want you to drive me insane with lust so that when you eventually put them on, I won't care. Make me submit to your bonds."

Okay. Georgina was a newbie—to his club, to kinky sex. Yet she offered him a gift even a pro would baulk at.

Was she high? Or drunk?

"Stay there." He pushed off the floor and reached for his phone on the low dark table.

"What's wrong?" she asked, face crumpled.

"How much of that alcohol did you drink?" He asked while he sent a message to the bar manager: *What did you serve my guest?*

"It's just a vodka and coke," she replied with a frown. "I didn't even finish it. You can check the glass on the sideboard."

He strode over there and raised the cup. It was half-filled with dark liquid and melting ice which he sniffed. Some clubbers requested a little extra with their drinks—poppers, blow, you name. It was all available at Arufin, in the VIP section. He didn't think she'd gotten that far—still, better safe than sorry.

His phone buzzed, and he checked the message from Rayo. *Vodka, coke, and ice.* It confirmed what was in the tumbler.

He put the phone away and turned to a frowning Georgina. "I have a strict 'no sex with alcohol' rule here, which also excludes any recreational drugs. Have you had any other substances tonight?"

"Of course not." She appeared affronted and turned on all fours, ready to push off the floor. "Maybe this was a bad idea."

"Not so fast." He lowered onto his knees behind her, leaning forward to cover her back. "The rule is meant to safeguard everyone. Trust me, you don't want a drunk or high person in charge of your pleasure any more than I want to harm you. Likewise, consent from a drunk or high individual is not consent."

He pressed a kiss between her shoulder blades.

Shivering, she moaned.

God help him. Her moan vibrated at the base of his spine. He thrust slowly against her bum cheeks, grunting as his cock thickened in his trousers.

"Does that mean you want to stop?" She glanced back, smiling, and biting her bottom lip as she rolled her hips provocatively.

Oh, she knew exactly what she was doing. Knew the effect she had on him. Knew how fucking hard he was.

He grunted and swallowed before he could find his thick husky voice, "Depends on if you're drunk. Are you drunk, sweetheart?"

He could dish out sweet torture too. He cupped her right breast, squeezed, and rolled the nipple.

"Ohhh," she gasped, arching her neck. "Not drunk on alcohol or drugs. But I'd like to get drunk on you."

"Then nothing other than your safe word is going to stop me." He tweaked her nipple again, loving her soft cries.

He needed more skin-to-skin contact. Easing onto his heels, he removed his cufflinks, unbuttoned his shirt, and pulled it off, along with his white vest. He tossed them on the back of a sofa.

Georgina rolled, sat on her bum, thighs spread, showing off the pretty black panties covering her pussy.

"Wow." She stared at the tattoos on his chest and arms. "These are stunning."

"You are the stunning one," he said, trailing his thumb across her chin. The tattoos told his life story and today wasn't the day to unveil them.

She reached for his trousers, unbuckling the belt, and tugging the zipper.

He never allowed anyone else to touch him like this, which was why they were usually cuffed. He should stop her. Inexplicably, he didn't.

She reached into his boxers, wrapped a warm palm around his thick girth and pulled him out. Precum dripped from the swollen tip. She scooped the white streaks, using it to jack him from root to end.

Head tipped back, he growled, fighting not to lose it before he'd started. "You're such a temptress."

She leaned in and whispered against his lips, "You bet I am."

He pounced on her, kissing her fiercely, crushing her body onto the carpet. His naked cock pushed against her knickers, his bare chest rubbing her breasts.

She wriggled and moaned, her pussy teasing his dick.

His body was on fire.

She wrapped her legs around his hips, making his cock grind against the edge of her black lace knickers and over her core.

He rolled his hips, grinding harder, making her squirm as he peppered her mouth, cheek, and neck with kisses.

The sound of her moans matched the baseline of the thumping music. He tugged her knickers to the side, making his tip glide over her smooth-shaven labia.

He hissed in pleasure and slipped his fingers between her thighs.

"Fuck. You're so wet. Dripping wet," he said in a husky voice, his fingers gliding over her glistening pussy.

"You make me so horny, babe." She lifted her hips, grinding herself against his hand.

He slid a finger inside her, stroked in and out.

Squeezing her eyes shut, she gripped his shoulders, increased her humping, writhing, and whimpering as he added more fingers and curved them to hit her sweet spot.

He shoved her bra aside, freeing her breasts for his mouth. He licked his way down the slope of her breasts to her hardened nipples, tasting salty skin.

She was everything he wanted in a woman, right this minute.

Her dripping arousal, her musical moans, her sweet taste, her bouncing body, absolutely perfect.

"That's it, sweetheart. Let go and fuck my hand. Take your pleasure from me."

There was nothing more beautiful, more erotic than seeing a woman abandon inhibitions and enjoy herself. The blissful expression on her face as she chased the orgasm was better than anything else.

He sucked a tender spot on her collarbone and returned to her neck, sucking, and nipping.

"Oh, oh, oh, oh, oh," her chanting filled the air.

His thumb pressed on her clit, his fingers surging in and out of her with her upwards thrusts.

Her body curled tight as her orgasm soared and she screamed his name, shuddering for seconds on end.

EIGHT

DID ORGASMS KILL or was she just delirious?

Gina lay on the carpeted floor in what looked like Osagie's private lounge, wearing nothing but askew sheer black lace panties and bra set. Yet, she floated in nirvana.

There were hundreds of people downstairs partying the night away. The music vibrated under her back.

Shouldn't she feel ashamed for having sex in such a public arena? For allowing Osagie to finger-fuck her and humping his hand to oblivion.

Gosh, he'd been amazing. His dark eyes burning, his masculine body pinning hers to the floor and his mouth trailing toe-curling kisses over her neck, chest, and breasts.

He knew exactly what to do, where to lick and touch. Even his dirty words had taken her to the edge.

She panted for air, shivering in ecstasy, the aftershock of the orgasm rippling through her. She moaned quietly, her skin tingling, mind hazing and heat melting through her.

He lay on the floor beside her, cocooning her. She felt the weight of his hefty dick twitching and pulsing against her quivering pussy, his precum trickling over her mound. At the same time, her panties were stretched obscenely to the side.

Jeez, she'd never done anything this vulgar, this crude. Yet she didn't want it to end.

"Sweetheart, sit up," Osagie's voice broke through her foggy mind.

"What?" Gina blinked several times, disorientated.

She must have drifted off to sleep, having not seen him move.

"Have a drink." He squatted beside her with a small bottle of water in his hand.

She pushed off her elbows. Her head swam, and she struggled to breathe.

"Georgina?" He sat next to her, hand on her back, tipping her head forward.

She inhaled and exhaled steadily until the dizziness subsided. She took the water from him and drank, emptying the 500ml bottle.

Osagie took the container when she finished, his brows wrinkled.

"I'm okay," she muttered, noticing his concerned expression.

He shook his head. "When did you eat last?"

She squeezed her face, trying to remember. "I had an omelette for breakfast."

She hadn't even finished it.

His frown deepened. "Lunch?"

She'd been upset and couldn't stomach anything at the time. Nigel had later offered dinner, but she didn't mention it. Osagie didn't like the man. She didn't want to ruin the mood.

She shook her head—bad idea. The dizzy spell returned.

"Fuck," Osagie swore and scooped his arms under her body, lifting her and carrying her to the sofa. "I'm taking you home."

She didn't argue as exhaustion hit her. "It's just low blood sugar. I usually carry energy bars in my tote when I'm out and about and can't stop for a meal. But I haven't had those for a week."

"I'm sorry. I should have known you hadn't eaten." His arms around her tightened, and he brushed his lips on her clammy forehead. "There's a suya place next door. I'll send Nekpen to buy some."

He leaned forward, picked his phone, and started typing.

She rubbed her cheek on his short chest hair, breathing in the familiar scent of man and cologne.

"You smell nice," she said, nuzzling his neck. She licked the dip of his collar and nipped his Adam's apple. She'd wanted him this close for so long. It was only a week, and yet she felt like she'd known him forever.

He groaned, his chest vibrating, his eyes closing briefly. "Sweetheart, behave."

"But I want you," she teased, loving his response to her touch. Loving that he didn't try to hide the way he felt. Pouting, she fluttered lashes and tilted her head, hoping to seduce him into finishing what they'd started.

"Don't look at me like that. No more orgasms for you until you eat." He looked away, shaking his head. The corner of his lips tugged in a half-smile.

"I hear semen is full of nutrients," she said with a straight face, trying a different tactic.

He jerked back, and his mouth flopped open in a flabbergasted expression.

She burst into laughter, her body shaking. "Oh, God. Your face."

He covered his face with both hands and leaned into the sofa. "I'm in so much trouble."

"Only the good kind, babe." She shifted position, straddling his thighs. Amazing how comfortable she felt in his company. Like they'd known each other for more than a week. She pressed hands on his shoulders and rolled hips over his groin.

He flipped her so fast, she didn't even see him move until her back was on the sofa cushion. "That's it. You're not getting another orgasm until after breakfast."

"Oh, no. What did I do?" She half-grumbled. "It's not my fault you make me horny."

"You're such a tease." Smiling, he shook his head and got off the sofa. He grabbed her clothes and placed them beside her. "Get dressed."

"You're no fun," she said without heat. She wanted him. But she also needed food. She'd burned more calories than usual without the nutrients to nourish her body.

He typed on his phone again while she pulled her clothes on.

She looked forward to getting home and not having to wear dirty clothes. She felt sticky and hot. But would have to wait until she could shower.

Interesting how she now referred to Osagie's house as home. When did the switch occur in her mind?

"Where's the bathroom?" she asked, needing space to think.

"Turn right in the hallway. It should be directly ahead." He pointed at the door and grabbed his shirt.

She followed his direction. The restroom had spotlights and shiny surfaces. She used the cubicle, washed her hands, and tidied her appearance in the mirror. With a little water, she brushed down her hair and retied the hairband.

Was she really doing this? Really about to go home with Osagie. Not just for a one-night stand. Not only as a casual hook-up.

What happened to not being ready for emotional entanglements?

Osagie had been adamant about being monogamous. And so was she. All those women waiting on the Star app would have an awfully long wait because she wouldn't give him up anytime soon. She hadn't made this kind of connection with a lover since...

Since never.

There were things about Osagie she would have to find out. Then again, they were not walking down the aisle. Oh, they were far off from wedding bells, and she wasn't getting married again. That resolve was still intact.

But she would take a lover. A steady, faithful, generous, compassionate, albeit dangerous lover.

She would take Osagie, and hopefully, with time, everything else would fall into place.

When she came out of the ladies', Osagie waited outside the lounge in the blue-lit corridor.

Looking as handsome as ever in his shirt and trousers, the jacket and tie flung over his arm, while he held a leather briefcase.

Her heart skipped a beat.

This was her man. She didn't know how it had happened. She hadn't thought she was ready for a steady lover. But she knew without a doubt that she wanted more from Osagie than just one night.

"You ready?" he asked as she stepped up to him.

"Yes, Mr Peters." She pressed a quick kiss to his lips. "So, what's the plan?"

"The plan is I feed you, get you home and unleash my surprise." His hand settled on the small of her back, and he steered her towards the lifts. He pressed the call button.

Her skin tingled where he touched. "Of course, the surprise. You mean it's still on."

"You bet it is." He grinned mysteriously as they stepped into the lift, piquing her interest.

A few seconds later they descended to the basement and the car park. The idling car was ready by the entrance.

Osagie held the door. She climbed in, and he joined her in the soft leather back seat. He removed the middle divider so she could lean against him.

"Welcome, Boss, Ma'am," the driver said.

"Nekpen, how are you?" she asked the man, cheerfully.

The executive car was luxurious, and she hadn't paid attention when she'd sat in it earlier. Really terrific how her life had changed in a few hours. When Osagie had forced her to leave Nigel's apartment, she'd thought he'd kill her. Now she was going home with him voluntarily.

"I'm okay, Madam. Here is the suya you wanted, Boss," Nekpen replied, reached into the front passenger seat, and lifted a paper bag.

Osagie opened it and took out the parcel wrapped in paper. "Here you go."

"Thank you." Gina unwrapped it, her mouth already watering at the aroma. She bit into a piece of peppery spiced grilled meat and moaned out loud. Her stomach rumbled.

Osagie grinned, pulling out a can of malt drink as Nekpen drove onto the road.

"Here, have a piece," she offered, lifting the pack with her left hand.

"Don't worry about me. The suya is for you." Osagie waved her off.

"Have you eaten?"

He shrugged. "I had lunch. I was meant to have dinner with you tonight."

Her chest tightened. They'd been sharing dinners together for the past week, a routine she missed today.

"Then let's share this." She lowered the middle rest and placed the parcel of suya on it. Then she lifted a piece of suya and held it in front of him.

He opened his mouth, his tongue flicked out and swiped her finger as well.

A tingle travelled through her. Her breath hitched.

He smiled, chewing with relish. He opened the cans of malt and handed one to her. They fed each other, making small talk while the car headed across town to Osagie's house in the Apata Peninsula.

Afterwards, he pulled a pack of wet wipes from the side panel. They cleaned their fingers and balled the wastepaper into the bag that Nekpen placed on the front seat.

"Let me be the first to wish you a Merry Christmas." Osagie raised a can.

"It's Christmas Day?"

"Yes. It's past midnight."

"Oh, wow." She'd totally forgotten about the day for the past few hours. At one point, she hadn't thought she'd live to see the 25th of December.

"Merry Christmas, sweetheart." He leaned across and pecked the corner of her mouth.

She twisted and kissed him thoroughly. "Merry Christmas, Mr Peters."

He lingered before leaning back, grinning. "Merry Christmas, Nekpen."

"Ehm." The driver coughed. "Merry Christmas, Boss."

Gina giggled. "Nekpen, you sound like it's the first time Osagie said Merry Christmas to you."

"Eh, madam…" The man seemed uncertain what to say and glanced at Osagie via the rear-view mirror.

Osagie grimaced. "You're correct. It's the first time in years I've said Merry Christmas to another adult. Things are different this year because of you."

Her throat locked tight, and tears clouded her eyes. Things are different for her too. Her mother wouldn't be here. Yet, the isolation she'd expected wasn't here. She wouldn't spend the day alone.

"It's going to be a great Christmas because of you." She reached across, lifted, and kissed the back of his hand.

He held onto her and pressed their joined hands to his lips. "Do you trust me?"

"Yes," she said without hesitation. She understood his capabilities. He was a principled man even if his methods weren't always straightforward. He'd always followed through on his promises.

"Thank you." He pressed his lips to her fingers. "I need you to close your eyes and don't open them until I tell you."

"Okay." She frowned.

"Don't be worried. I promise it's nothing bad. Go on, close them."

She did, and he held her hand.

The car slowed down. She figured they were near Osagie's residence.

The clanking of gates confirmed it.

Her heart raced. What did he have in store for her?

The car rolled over gravel and stopped.

She licked her lips in excitement. "Can I open my eyes now?"

He chuckled and a few seconds later purred in her ear. "You can open them now."

Gina lifted her lids, and the glow shocked her into squinting. Gradually she widened her eyes.

"Oh, my God!" Her mouth dropped open.

The house's front width was bedecked in staggered, waterfall fairy lights covering the first and ground levels. It looked like she was outside a magical Christmas grotto.

"Wow."

The car door opened, and Nathaniel stood there beaming a smile. "Madam, welcome home."

"Thank you," she said and stepped out, breath stalled. It was even more fantastic standing in the shimmery glow. "But how did you do this?"

When she'd left here around lunchtime, none of this was up.

Osagie came to stand beside her. "This was the errand I sent Nathaniel. I wanted you out of the house and Idehen was meant to keep you in the mall for a few hours. It was meant to be a surprise for you when you came back after shopping."

"You planned this?" her voice choked, and tears clogged her eyes. He'd really meant to surprise her.

He nodded, giving her the most gorgeous smile. "There's more inside."

"More? I want to see it." She couldn't help the excited squeal in her voice. Blood rushed in her ears as she ran up the short stairs onto the portico.

A poinsettia and baubles wreath hung on the open front door. Garlands hung around the narrow table in the foyer and more garlands curled around the balustrades leading upstairs. Flashing lights drew her to the spacious living room.

She gasped.

Fairy lights, garlands, tinsels, wrapped presents and a huge, decorated Christmas tree almost touched the ceiling.

Okay. Gina had to be dreaming. When Osagie had said he had a surprise for her, she'd thought he meant sex. Not this.

This was the best Christmas surprise she could imagine.

She covered her face with her hands as tears clouded her eyes.

"Are you okay?" Osagie said quietly behind her.

She swivelled and walked into his arms, burying her face in his neck, and inhaling his warm scent.

"Did I do something wrong?" he asked, sounding concerned, wrapping his arms around her.

"No, babe." She lifted her head, smiling through blurry eyes. "You did the most wonderful thing."

He had a frown on his face and swiped a tear with his thumb. "So why are you crying?"

"I'm not sad. It's just... I didn't think this year's Christmas would be this joyful. All the decorations reminded me of spending this time with my parents. I miss them."

She'd spoken to him about her late parents. He'd been attentive and sympathetic.

"I know, sweetheart." He caressed her cheek. "I know I can never make up for their absence. But I wanted to try, so I have another surprise. I hope you don't mind."

"Another surprise? This is pretty amazing." She glanced around the shimmery living room.

He stepped to the side, revealing the living room door where her sister stood quietly, smiling.

Gina's heart slammed, and she clutched her chest. "Dani!"

The two sisters hurried across the room and embraced each other.

"How are you here? You were supposed to go back to Highgate," Gina asked, stepping back to look at her sister as they settled into a sofa.

Dani had changed from what she'd been wearing earlier this evening. She wore a black and white print jumpsuit with the tie knotted at the waist and high-heeled sandals. Her wavy ginger tresses loose on her shoulders and face made-up. Always glam, she looked like she was attending a party.

"Idehen took me home. Then said I had to come here with him. So, I showered and changed and got back in the car. I was supposed to pack an overnight bag, but I just brought the suitcase from my trip," Dani said.

"Overnight bag? You're staying?" Gina looked at Osagie, who had a sheepish grin on his face.

"I want you here for Christmas. But I thought you'd also like to spend the day with your sister. I had planned to bring her here from the airport. But..." He shrugged.

Stunned, her mouth dropped open.

He had planned to bring her sister to his house before she'd run away. He'd been thoughtful and considerate, something she'd never expected from a man like him.

She got off the sofa and walked over to him, wrapping her arms around his neck before whispering against his mouth, "Thank you."

Then she kissed him, slowly and yet full of gratitude and yearning.

He held her close, angling his head and deepening the kiss.

He didn't know precisely what he'd done for her. Inadvertently, he'd fulfilled her Christmas wish. He couldn't bring back her parents, but he'd given her the next best thing, a new family of sorts.

"Get a room." Dani coughed.

Gina lifted her head, smiling. "We're going."

She turned to her sister. "Right. Sorry, I'm going to leave you. I'm sure Nathaniel will show you to your room for the night. But I need to go show my babe how grateful I am. I'll see you in the morning. Good night."

"Oh. I've already seen the room. I'm cool. Good night."

"Come on," Gina dragged Osagie back into the foyer and up the stairs. "Which one is your bedroom?"

"This." He opened the door.

The bedroom was massive with cream walls and a king-size bed in the middle. The only lights were the low string lights draped over the curtain rails, making the place glow and cosy.

She turned to him. "You blew my mind today. So, I'm going to blow your mind."

"No, no, no, sweetheart. I told you no more orgasms for you tonight." Grinning, he leaned against the wall.

"I heard you. But nothing stops me from making you come, Mr Peters." She winked.

He chuckled and palmed his face. "I should've seen that coming. You always find every loophole. You should have been a lawyer."

"Yep. It's something I picked from my dad." She dismissed the pang in her chest and stepped back. "Anyway, I feel hot and sticky, so I'm going to shower, change into something comfortable and join you shortly."

"You know you can use my bathroom."

"I know, but my things are in the other room. See you soon."

"I'll be waiting." He stood at the door, watching as she moved backwards then turned and hurried to the room she'd been staying in.

In the ensuite, she turned on the shower faucet, and steam filled the room as she stripped off the clothes. Leaving them on the bathroom floor. She wrapped her hair into a tight bun, covered it with a shower cap and entered the enclosure. The warm water teased her skin before she applied the orange and cinnamon scented shower gel onto the loofah. She scrubbed her body, shaved her legs and pussy.

Then she switched off the shower, grabbed a fluffy white towel and dried her body.

Her nipples hardened in anticipation and her clit throbbed, heat already pooled in her core.

Body dried, she applied body cream to her elbows, knees, hands, and feet. It was a warm Harmattan night. The joints dried out quickly so needed moisture, but she also wanted to stay cool. She pulled on the short burgundy silk nightie and matching robe.

Then she headed across the hall to Osagie's bedroom, tapped on the slab.

The door opened. A towel-clad Osagie tugged her, shut the door, and slammed his lips against hers.

She wrapped her arms and legs around him, moaning into his mouth.

Bulging arms lifted her, and his hands cupped her bum cheeks as he carried her further into the room, their kissing frenzied. He deposited her onto the soft bed and followed her down, pressing hard chest against her body and chasing her mouth.

"Somebody missed me," she teased, running her palms along his shoulders, legs wrapped around his naked hips. The towel must have slipped off.

"I sure did. That seemed to be the longest wait of my life, even if it was only thirty minutes." He nibbled her earlobe, his hands slipping under her negligee onto her skin.

Her breath hitched. "You were timing me?"

"Only because I checked the time before I went into the shower. Whatever you did for thirty minutes, you smell divine, and your skin is amazing. I can't stop touching and tasting."

As if to prove it, he licked her neck and nipped her collar.

She moaned again and shoved his chest. "Before I get lost and forget who's being blown. Lie on your back and shift up the bed."

He didn't waste time and shuffled up the mattress, head to the pillows. He looked regal and masculine, thighs spread, a grin on his face as she tossed her robe and nightie.

Completely naked, rigid muscles, scars, and mesmerising tattoo ink. He looked sexy as hell, the screen-worthy jawline and strong cheekbones, the sensuous lips and chiselled body, the silver and onyx hair on his chin and head. His chest expanded with a long inhale.

She could stay here all night and watch him. Instead, she climbed and settled between his legs.

"I've left these here, in case you wanted any of them." He waved at the bedside cabinet. There was a pack of flavoured condoms, lube, and sex toys.

"Maybe later. Let me taste you first."

She wrapped her palm around his thick dick, lowered her mouth and went to town on him, licking and sucking.

He groaned, eyes closing, hand wresting on her hair while the other caressed her shoulder.

Arousal flooded her, and her pussy throbbed. She hummed, pumping her head up and down and working him with her hand.

His grip on her head tightened and his sounds of pleasure deepened. His breathing quickened. "Sweetheart, mercy."

She lifted her head, pulling her mouth off his glistening cock. "What would you like, Mr Peters?"

His eyes were wild, intense, and he groaned. "I want my mouth on your pussy."

"Nah. Objections, my lord. I want your dick in my pussy."

"Objections sustained, counsellor."

Grinning, she rose to her knees and straddled his hips. Slowly, she lowered her body onto him. He was snug and thick and hard, stretching her insides. Her breath hitched, and she bit her bottom lips. Fingers raking his chest, she started riding him.

"*Fuck*, sweetheart," he growled, hands skimming her smooth thighs and hips, eyes blazing. "Feels good to be inside you."

"Feels awesome, babe." She rocked back and forth, gently at first, like a bronco rider feeling their way. She was breathless, body hot, heart pounding.

He didn't even try to take over. Happy to lie there and let her ride him. Another thing about this man that she was getting to love. He was so freaking confident about himself, he didn't have to jostle for a position of power. He didn't have to prove anything to her.

Here they were. Their first proper time together and he'd allowed her to be on top to control the outcome.

Never mind that she loved this position because she was guaranteed an orgasm. Although she'd said this was his treat.

He stretched across, grabbed something from the table. Then he reached between them and parted her labia. The object in his hand—the bullet—vibrated against her clit.

"Ohhhhhh," she let out a long moan of pleasure, body arching, head tilted, eyes rolling back.

Her movement went wild and fast, her sounds of delight increasing. Her breasts bounced, her body undulating and rocking.

"That's it, sweetheart—" he groaned "—ride my dick—" he exhaled "—ride me hard."

His voice was guttural, animalistic, his hips snapping upwards as his grip on her tightened.

Eyes locked, they moved in sync, both panting, making sounds of pleasure that filled the room. No one else mattered. No one else existed except the two of them.

His eyes were on her, the vibe still on her clit, buzzing away, driving her towards the peak. He lifted the other hand, cupped her face, and leaned forwards. She lowered her head and kissed him. With everything in her, swallowing his groans as he swallowed hers. Their bodies writhing against each other.

Pressure built. The wave of climax rushed in. Her pussy clenched tightly around his dick, and a heatwave swarmed her veins.

He grunted and kept thrusting as she detonated in ecstasy, vision blurring, body trembling. "Babe, oh. Oh. Ohhhh."

Her rippling inside walls seemed to drag his orgasm out. He drove deep into her and grunted. His dick throbbed and pulsed inside her.

Their tongues duelled, bodies grinding together. Their hands gripped each other tightly as wave after wave of orgasm flowed through them.

Osagie kissed her passionately and rolled her to the side, her legs still wrapped around his hips.

He stroked his palms down her face and back tenderly.

"That was amazing," she whispered against his mouth.

"Absolutely. Stay right there." He rolled off the bed, strode into the bathroom and returned with a towel, with which he cleaned her. He tossed it aside and climbed into bed, tugging the sheet over them. He stroked his palm over her skin.

"You are the best Christmas present I've had in years," he said.

"Oh. But I didn't buy you anything." A guilty pang went through her. He'd done so much for her.

"All I wanted for Christmas was you, and you're here. So, thank you."

"And you gave me a fantastic gift as well. My sister is here. You are here. And we're all going to be together. You can't top that."

"How about I write off your sister's debt?"

Her eyes widened. "You'd do that?"

He cupped her cheek. "I would. For you."

She leaned forward and kissed him briefly. "Thank you. That's generous. But instead of forgiving the total debt, can you write off the interest. That way, she only pays back the original amount stolen. My sister needs to understand personal responsibility and consequences. If she gets away with theft this time, she'll do it again."

She knew Dani too well. She'd done it before.

"Fair enough." He sighed, still stroking her arm. "I know the way we met wasn't ideal. But I hope you'll stay."

"Of course I'll stay. No more running away." She replied, kissing him.

Soon kisses turned to passion, and he proceeded to worship her again.

EPILOGUE

AFTER BREAKFAST on Christmas Day, the entire new Peters household—Osagie, Gina, Dani and Idehen, and staff—drove to the Itohan Peters Children's' Home where Osagie played the visiting Father Christmas, a role he alternated with Idehen biannually.

Dressed in his red suit, robe, and hat, he sat in a little grotto and gave wrapped presents to each resident child. The gifts had been purchased from donations of which Osagie and Idehen were significant contributors as patrons.

Stunned at Osagie's generosity, and big heart, Gina had only fallen deeper in love with him.

Afterwards, they returned to Osagie's house for Christmas dinner, a wonderful meal prepared by Nathaniel. They all sat at the eight-seat table—Osagie, Gina, Idehen, Dani, Nathaniel,

Nekpen and the two security men. The first time, apparently.

But Gina had insisted that everyone in the household would eat Christmas dinner together. A tradition her parents had instilled in her.

Boxing Day, Gina went to her apartment briefly to pick up some items. She spent the rest of the week with Osagie in his house.

On New Year's Eve, they attended the Odili's dinner party as a couple.

Thank you for reading Osagie: Bad Santa. Please leave a review if you can.

Gina and Osagie are back later in the Yadili series in **Osagie: King of Clubs**.

Want more? Scan the QR code to receive bonus content.

Visit www.kirutaye.com and sign up to Kiru's newsletter to receive book news via email. Join her forum for freebies and exclusive sneak peeks.

YADILI SERIES

<u>Prince of Hearts</u>
<u>Killer of Kings</u>
<u>Bad Santa</u>
<u>Rough Diamond</u>
<u>Tough Alliance</u>

Keep reading for a sneak preview at Rough Diamond, Yadili series #4

ROUGH DIAMOND – CHAPTER ONE

Ten years ago

A week after his father was buried, Mason Maduka was on the hunt for pussy.

Not the animal.

But the part of the female anatomy designed to take a pounding.

Because it was what he needed. Rough, rugged, bed-quaking sex to make him forget, if only for a little while, that he'd buried his most favourite person in the world seven goddamned days ago.

Hence he sat on a leather couch in this dimly lit lounge while thumping Afrobeat music rattled the graffiti-covered walls and water-stained ceiling.

Women in little more than lingerie lined up in front of him. They varied in size—slender and plump, short and tall, young and not-so-young.

Prostitutes, one and all.

Or sex workers, as they were termed these days.

He liked the newer phrase. An apt label—clear and concise. No danger of mistaking it for something else.

No way to mistake what these ladies of the night were offering. They fluttered lashes coquettishly, plumped up boobs, jiggled arses, and pouted their lips, all vying for his attention.

They were preaching to the converted.

Mason hadn't experienced sexual pleasure since receiving news of his father's death six months ago. So, he was raring to go. Excitement flushed his skin, and he darted out his tongue, licking his lips.

The atmosphere of danger and dingy darkness spiked his heart rate and sent blood rushing to his dick. The prospect of trouble thrilled him as much as the nearly naked women did. He'd driven over an hour to the city slum for these exact reasons—peril and pussy.

He could get pussy closer to home, but tonight he needed extra, some recklessness to tip him over the brink.

These women were up for anything. Would accept anything for a monetary price.

This suited him perfectly because all sex was transactional. The people who didn't demand cash for sex still taxed their partners in other ways, mainly in the form of relationships. Relationships sucked time and energy, which amounted to money. So, every sexual encounter had a financial implication. He would rather pay it up front and walk away at the end.

He'd fucked a few of his neighbourhood girls. Nevertheless, navigating the respectability involved in courting middle-class brats whose parents would show up at his doorstep because he stole their daughter's cherry and broke her heart was a nightmare. Or worse, the ones who wanted to snap photos together and post them online, claiming they were in a relationship with him. Never mind that he could never fully express his deviant desires with those local women. In other words, messing with them proved unfulfilling.

So, it had been revelatory when for his eighteenth birthday, his older brother Rocha gifted him a Runs Girl, a woman willing to get with him purely for the financial rewards. A terrific alternative. From then on, his sexual interactions changed, and he always negotiated the fee upfront before he fucked anyone.

Hence his ease around hookers. He loved the transactional nature of the encounters because they were clear and concise. Requirements laid out, there lay no room for misunderstandings. Satisfaction for the control freak in him.

So, yes, he was in his element, right here and now.

A deep inhalation drew stale air, cigarette smoke, and weed aroma into his nostrils. He could light up, too, but he didn't like being stoned. He hated having his senses dulled or being out of control. He wanted to feel everything, pain and pleasure.

Otherwise, what was the point?

Indeed, why was he procrastinating, delaying his selection? Any one of these women should do the job. Then again, he had specific requirements.

He eyed the woman with locs and nipple rings showing through her white crop top. A tattoo snaked down her belly, disappearing into her black lace knickers. It would have been excruciatingly uncomfortable when it was inked. Anyone who purposely punctured their genitalia region with needles would like pain, undoubtedly, which suited his needs.

"Her. Tattoo girl." He indicated with his index finger. She was heavily made-up, which wasn't his cup of tea. But he didn't care as long as the rest of her assets were functional.

The beefy man standing in the shadows nodded at the woman who sauntered over. The rest disappeared into the corridor, barely masking their disappointments.

Mason patted the cushion beside him.

With a smile, Tattoo Girl lowered her slender body on the sofa and placed a hand on his lap. "You want to go to the room?"

He grabbed her wrist and twisted her arm. Not enough to injure her but hurting sufficiently to cause discomfort.

Her face twisted in a grimace as she gasped. She slipped off the sofa and landed on her knees to relieve the pressure. She looked up, pupils dilated, mouth slackened.

Oh, she enjoyed pain. The sadist in him cheered, and his dick hardened.

"What's your name?" he asked in a firm tone, not releasing her arm, keeping her on her knees.

"Jet, sir," she replied, puffing out a heavy breath.

A sizzle went down his spine, the sensation weird and yet pleasing.

He would be twenty-six years old in a few months, and she should be in her late thirties, if not forties. So, her addressing him as 'sir' should make him feel old.

Instead, it gave him a hard-on.

In a country where old age was exalted over youth and old people without wisdom or maturity frequently cruelly lorded over the young, this was his way of flipping the tables.

To have someone who would otherwise demand to be addressed with reverence on her knees about to service him?

Yes! He felt powerful. Respected.

"Respect is earned by action alone," his late father's words played in his mind.

Without thought, his hand clenched tightly around the woman's arm, and her breath hitched. He loosened his grip and leaned back in the leather seat. His father's words, while helpful, were not suitable for this moment. He shoved it aside and focused on the reason he was there.

"Jet," he said. "I ask the questions. If I need you to do anything, I'll tell you. Understood?"

"Yes, sir." She nodded but didn't move from the floor.

He gestured for the man in the shadows to draw the wooden partition, secluding their section. He didn't want to go to a room since there was a high likelihood of a camera being set up there. Not that he had a problem exhibiting himself. But he would rather it wasn't recorded without his permission.

Then again, there was his family's reputation to consider if the photos went public. He'd travelled this distance to an environment outside his circles and family's influence, partially for anonymity.

"Think about your family," his mother's words played in his mind.

What the fuck? Now, he needed to remember something his brother said, and he would require a stint in a psychiatric hospital.

He was seriously screwed up if he couldn't concentrate on the woman and get lost in pussy like he intended.

"Strip off your clothes and suck my dick," he said in a growly voice.

The woman's mouth and naked body should distract him from his unwelcome thoughts.

She shuffled forward, pulling her top off and exposing her breasts. Then she shoved her panties and manoeuvred to pull them from her legs.

He widened his legs, undoing his belt buckle. Then he leaned forward, pulled the string of flavoured condom packs from his back pocket, and placed them beside him. Next, he reached into his boxer briefs, tugged his semi out, and pumped it a few times until it filled out and hardened before rolling a condom on.

She watched him, licking her lips as if she couldn't wait to taste his erection.

He grabbed her head roughly and shoved it down onto his dick. She choked as the breath left her lungs, and he pulled her up and repeated the action until she got used to the rhythm he wanted. Then, he loosened his grip and allowed her to do her job.

He reached down and tugged at her nipple rings repeatedly, causing her to moan and writhe each time. The blowjob was okay, but she enjoyed it more than he did. Minutes ticked by, and he couldn't reach release or shake the lingering grief constricting his chest.

On the verge of deflating, he pulled out of her mouth and flipped her onto her stomach. Hand on her nape, he shoved her face to the carpet. Then he lined up his dick and slammed into her. Gripping her neck tightly and roughly, he rammed into her repeatedly, his belt buckle digging into her skin with each slam.

She didn't complain, loving the pain. Instead, her moans filled the space, and her body soon quaked with multiple orgasms.

Still, no luck for him, release proving elusive.

Frustrated, he pulled out and sank heavily into the sofa.

"Make I finish am." She reached for him.

"Don't touch me," he growled, smacking her hand away and standing instead.

He rolled the condom off, wiped himself with some tissues and stuffed his partially erect dick away, tidying himself up.

He pulled an envelope out of his wallet. Although he'd already paid upfront before he made his selection, there was no reason he shouldn't tip the woman. She'd done her job. The problem was in his head.

"For you." He dropped the cash on the sofa and headed towards the exit.

"Thank you," she called out behind him.

He didn't turn, ignoring her as he entered the dark corridor with oily blue walls lit by fluorescent bulbs. A man stood by the door, smoking weed. One of the gangsters who ran the brothel. He'd been in that exact position when Mason went in about an hour ago. He nodded at Mason as he exited the dingy building.

"Ashawo, give me my money!"

Mason heard the racket as soon as he stepped outside, away from the thumping music.

The sense of danger returned, sending a thrill through him. Like the flick of a switch, his pulse rate accelerated, and adrenaline rushed through him.

He'd witnessed street fights before and had never butted in. If someone was going to pick a fight, they better be ready to defend themselves or take what was coming to them.

It had been a week since his dead father was buried, and he was hurting. Hurting to unleash the ball of rage in his gut. Hurting to be used as a punching bag. Hurting to inflict pain and to receive enough physical pain to mask the emotional ones. He'd attempted sex, but it hadn't worked. He was still a keg of dynamite waiting to explode.

Why had his father gone so soon? His old man had been diagnosed with bowel cancer, and within a month, he was dead. Mason had been away at Law School. His family hadn't informed him until it was too late. He hadn't had time to say goodbye. To tell his father he loved him. To listen to the man tell him stories of his youthful exploits one last time.

The second of two sons, Mason had been closest to his father, his favourite person in the world, until his death. The old man had been strict but fair, a hands-on father. Sure, he'd worked long hours, but he'd shown up whenever Mason had needed him.

"Why should I give you all my money? I do the fucking work."

The defiance in the woman's angry voice roused Mason from his melancholy, and he surveyed the scene before him.

The sun had set, and the area was poorly lit with broken streetlights. Lamps were attached to the outside walls of some of the dilapidated single-storey buildings. The only multi-level structure was the one he had recently exited. The road was in such a state of disrepair the tarmac had utterly broken down, leaving jagged edges and crater-sized potholes. No demarcated pavements existed between the residences and the road, only open gutters covered with metal or concrete slabs at building entrances to provide walkways or driveways.

Several wooden stalls lit with kerosene lamps stood outside the houses, selling wares from basic groceries to cooked meals.

However, no one was purchasing anything. Instead, a crowd had gathered in the middle of the street, their attention focusing on the quarrelling couple. Enthralled and silent as if they were watching an outdoor theatre performance.

A huge, balding man in a black shirt and a pair of green trousers held a girl's throat. Petite in height, she wore a fitted black blouse stretching over her bountiful boobs and tapering at the waist. The undone buttons of her top revealed her flat stomach. White hotpants hugged her wide hips and barely concealed her ass, while smooth legs led to the white fake-leather wedge sandals on her feet. Loose, straight black braids partially obscured her face, making her appear wild as she glared at the man strangling her. But she seemed no older than Mason from this distance.

Her boldness and bravery ensnared him. Intrigued him.

For the first time in months, he forgot his loss, his grief. His despair. Instead of heading home, he stayed rooted, watching as if he'd joined the theatre audience, wondering how she would extricate herself from the situation. Taller than most in the crowd, he could see proceedings above their heads as if he were in an amphitheatre.

"Give me my fucking money!"

Mr Green Trousers smacked the girl across the face, the sharp sound of flesh against flesh unmistakable.

Mason flinched, shocked by the violent reminder. This wasn't a fictional street performance. This was reality.

It was one thing for a couple to shout at each other publicly. Quite another when it turned physical, especially when they were unevenly matched.

However, no one intervened to protect the girl. Like this was a regular occurrence. Just another piece of morbid entertainment. Just another means of escaping their miserable lives for a few minutes.

Disgust and anger rolled through him. His hands clenched and unclenched.

How could these people stand by and watch a man beat up a woman? How could they do nothing when the disparate power dynamic was so evident?

They reminded him of a similar crowd from long ago. A group who'd punished a victim by doing nothing.

Evil prevails when good people do nothing.

Not that Mason considered himself a good person. Yet, he couldn't be a bystander any longer. There was a pounding in his ears, and his throat dried out as he rushed his breaths.

Shoving men aside, he marched through the gathering, his mind set on a new purpose. He'd come to this slum for rough sex to ease his grief. Now, it seemed he would bloody his knuckles.

Adrenaline tingled through his veins as he yanked Mr Green Trousers' shoulder. "Leave her alone."

The man turned, snarling. "Small boy, waka pass. You know who I be?"

He was beefy, older, and in his forties. Eyes cold and deadly. He could beat Mason to a pulp.

However, with zero concerns, Mason felt reckless.

Desperate to feel something other than overwhelming grief, he was prepared to take a beating if it happened. Prepared to dish out some pain too. He flexed his muscles in preparation for a fight. "I don't care who you are. Just leave her the fuck alone."

"You dey mad?" The man swivelled, shoving the girl aside.

Mason didn't wait for the man to charge. Instead, he allowed six months of rage to flow through him. Taking a quick half-step backwards, he fluidly raised his left leg and landed a front kick into the man's groin.

The man grunted and grabbed his crotch, eyes bulging in unexpected pain.

Mason followed up with a jab and a hook, fists connecting with flesh and bone. The man toppled, face-planting on the road. Out cold.

The emotional constriction in Mason's chest eased. The man deserved a dose of his own medicine.

Wincing, the young woman pushed off the ground and stomped on the man's back. "Bastard!"

She turned to Mason with the most ridiculous smile he'd ever seen, blood dripping from her nose. Not exactly what he expected to see from someone being choked to death only minutes earlier.

"Thank you," she said, still smiling and wincing. "You for leave me, make I beat am, well well. I just dey prepare myself."

Surprisingly, he chuckled for the first time in months because she claimed she would've beaten up Mr Green Trousers any minute. Brave that she could find humour in her situation.

"No need to thank me. It was the only way I could get to where I was going. You guys were in my path." He spoke wryly as he stepped over the prone man and continued his journey.

The crowd seemed stunned into inaction, frozen to the spot as they gaped at the Mason. They hadn't expected him to survive the encounter. Best to keep moving.

The adrenaline in his veins ebbed, his rage de-escalating, allowing him to reason. He was far from home without friends or backup. Not that he liked an entourage, but they were sometimes necessary.

"In your path, eh. So where exactly are you going?" The girl grabbed her handbag from the ground and followed him, half laughing and half coughing.

He shrugged and continued walking but stopped when she kept shadowing him. "You should go to a hospital. You're injured."

"Hospital?" She laughed-coughed again, wiping her bloody nose with the seam of her top. "So, some quack doctor can take my hard-earned money. I don't think so. It's nothing that won't heal with time."

He could only imagine why she would have an aversion to medical doctors. Perhaps the ones in the slums were no good. He had news for her—some of the medics in the posh areas were bad too.

"Go home and rest, then," he said instead. She must be exhausted and in pain.

"Home? Are you kidding me? The place I stayed belongs to Bomba over there. Can you imagine what he will do to me when he wakes up? No. I'm not staying to find out. Everything I own is in this bag." She lifted the fake leather tote slung over her shoulder.

Confusion warred with disbelief. How could all her belongings fit in one bag? Sure, she was a hooker who lived in the slums. But she would have clothes, shoes, and personal effects, wouldn't she?

He frowned as his chest tightened. "Don't you have friends or relatives you can stay with?"

She rolled her eyes heavenwards as if the concept was ridiculous.

"You think if I had friends or family nearby, I would live with a pimp? I go find hotel. Somewhere wey cheap, sha. But not in this neighbourhood because Bomba and his friends will find me. So, I am following you. No one else around here was brave enough to stand against him. So right now, you're my security."

She flashed her pearly white teeth at him again with bravado. Yet, a longing in her tone echoed the intense ache suddenly welling inside his chest. He understood what it felt like to be isolated even when surrounded by people, a sensation hovering around him for the past six months.

"Oh." Mason rubbed his shaved chin, suppressing the unwanted emotion. He hadn't come here to play the Good Samaritan or pick up strays. Yet, he couldn't abandon her. "What's your name?"

She tilted her head to the side, and her voice softened. "People call me Sophie. And you?"

"I'm Mason. I'll get you to a hotel." He would get her somewhere safe tonight and leave her to sort herself out thereafter. Unfortunately, he lacked the emotional capacity to handle her problems. He had his own demons to wrangle.

"Then we better hurry because Bomba's boys are coming," she replied, jogging ahead.

He glanced back to find a group of men about fifty metres away, heading in his direction. Heart racing, he started running. The men gave chase, footsteps pounding on the road.

Find out more and sign up for LAP book news:
www.loveafricapress.com/newsletter

www.ingramcontent.com/pod-product-compliance
Lightning Source LLC
Chambersburg PA
CBHW020810190726